Adopting An Abandoned Farm

Kate Sanborn

Alpha Editions

This Edition Published in 2021

ISBN: 9789354599491

Design and Setting By
Alpha Editions
www.alphaedis.com
Email – info@alphaedis.com

As per information held with us this book is in Public Domain. This book is a reproduction of an important historical work. Alpha Editions uses the best technology to reproduce historical work in the same manner it was first published to preserve its original nature. Any marks or number seen are left intentionally to preserve its true form.

TABLE OF CONTENTS

CHAPTER I
FROM GOTHAM TO GOOSEVILLE — 1 -

CHAPTER II
AUCTIONS — 5 -

CHAPTER III
BUYING A HORSE — 13 -

CHAPTER IV
FOR THOSE WHO LOVE PETS — 19 -

CHAPTER V
STARTING A POULTRY FARM — 25 -

CHAPTER VI
GHOSTS — 32 -

CHAPTER VII
DAILY DISTRACTIONS — 40 -

CHAPTER VIII
THE PROSE OF NEW ENGLAND FARM LIFE — 45 -

CHAPTER IX
THE PASSING OF THE PEACOCKS — 54 -

CHAPTER X
LOOKING BACK — 65 -

CHAPTER I
FROM GOTHAM TO GOOSEVILLE

I have now come to the farmer's life, with which I am exceedingly delighted, and which seems to me to belong especially to the life of a wise man.

CICERO.

Weary of boarding at seashore and mountain, tired of traveling in search of comfort, hating hotel life, I visited a country friend at Gooseville, Conn. (an assumed name for Foxboro, Mass.), and passed three happy weeks in her peaceful home.

Far away at last from the garish horrors of dress, formal dinners, visits, and drives, the inevitable and demoralizing gossip and scandal; far away from hotel piazzas, with their tedious accompaniments of corpulent dowagers, exclusive or inquisitive, slowly dying from too much food and too little exercise; ennuied spinsters; gushing buds; athletic collegians, cigarettes in mouths and hands in pockets; languid, drawling dudes; old bachelors, fluttering around the fair human flower like September butterflies; fancy work, fancy work, like Penelope's web, never finished; pug dogs of the aged and asthmatic variety. Everything there but MEN—they are wise enough to keep far away.

Before leaving this haven of rest, I heard that the old-fashioned farmhouse just opposite was for sale. And, as purchasers of real estate were infrequent at Gooseville, it would be rented for forty dollars a year to any responsible tenant who would "keep it up."

After examining the house from garret to cellar and looking over the fields with a critical eye, I telegraphed to the owner, fearful of losing such a prize, that I would take it for three years. For it captivated me. The cosy "settin'-room," with a "pie closet" and an upper tiny cupboard known as a "rum closet" and its pretty fire place—bricked up, but capable of being rescued from such prosaic "desuetude"; a large sunny dining-room, with a brick oven, an oven suggestive of brown bread and baked beans—yes, the baked beans of my childhood, that adorned the breakfast table on a Sunday morning, cooked with just a little molasses and a square piece of crisp salt pork in center, a dish to tempt a dying anchorite.

There wore two broad landings on the stairs, the lower one just the place for an old clock to tick out its impressive "Forever—Never—Never—Forever" *à la* Longfellow. Then the long "shed chamber" with a wide swinging door opening to the west, framing a sunset gorgeous enough to inspire a mummy. And the attic, with its possible treasures.

There was also a queer little room, dark and mysterious, in the center of house on the ground floor, without even one window, convenient to retire to during severe thunder storms or to evade a personal interview with a burglar; just the place, too, for a restless ghost to revisit.

Best of all, every room was blessed with two closets.

Outside, what rare attractions! Twenty-five acres of arable land, stretching to the south; a grand old barn, with dusty, cobwebbed, hay-filled lofts, stalls for two horses and five cows; hen houses, with plenty of room to carry out a long-cherished plan of starting a poultry farm.

The situation, too, was exceptional, since the station from which I could take trains direct to Boston and New York almost touched the northern corner of the farm, and nothing makes one so willing to stay in a secluded spot as the certainty that he or she can leave it at any time and plunge directly into the excitements and pleasures which only a large city gives.

What charmed me most of all was a tiny but fascinating lakelet in the pasture near the house; a "spring-hole" it was called by the natives, but a lakelet it was to me, full of the most entrancing possibilities. It could be easily enlarged at once, and by putting a wind-mill on the hill, by the deep pool in "Chicken Brook" where the pickerel loved to sport, and damming something, somewhere, I could create or evolve a miniature pond, transplant water lilies, pink and white, set willow shoots around the well-turfed, graveled edge, with roots of the forget-me-not hiding under the banks their blue blossoms; just the flower for happy lovers to gather as they lingered in their rambles to feed my trout. And there should be an arbor, vine-clad and sheltered from the curious gaze of the passers-by, and a little boat, moored at a little wharf, and a plank walk leading up to the house. And—and oh, the idealism possible when an enthusiastic woman first rents a farm—an "abandoned" farm!

It may be more exact to say that my farm was not exactly "abandoned," as its owner desired a tenant and paid the taxes; say rather depressed, full of evil from long neglect, suffering from lack of food and general debility.

As "abandoned farms" are now a subject of general interest, let me say that my find was nothing unusual. The number of farms without occupants in New Hampshire in August, 1889, was 1,342 and in Maine 3,318; and I saw lately a farm of twenty acres advertised "free rent and a present of fifty dollars."

But it is my farm I want you to care about. I could hardly wait until winter was over to begin my new avocation. By the last of March I was assured by practical agriculturists (who regarded me with amusement tempered with pity) that it was high time to prune the lazy fruit trees and arouse, if possible, the debilitated soil—in short, begin to "keep it up."

So I left New York for the scene of my future labors and novel lessons in life, accompanied by a German girl who proved to be merely an animated onion in matters of cooking, a half-breed hired man, and a full-bred setter pup who suffered severely from nostalgia and strongly objected to the baggage car and separation from his playmates.

If wit is, as has been averred, the "juxtaposition of dissimilar ideas," then from "Gotham to Gooseville" is the most scintillating epigram ever achieved. Nothing was going on at Gooseville except time and the milk wagon collecting for the creamery. The latter came rumbling along every morning at 4.30 precisely, with a clatter of cans that never failed to arouse the soundest sleeper.

The general dreariness of the landscape was depressing. Nature herself seemed in a lethargic trance, and her name was mud.

But with a house to furnish and twenty-five enfeebled acres to resuscitate, one must not mind. Advanced scientists assure us of life, motion, even intelligence, appetite, and affection in the most primitive primordial atoms. So, after a little study, I found that the inhabitants of Gooseville and its outlying hamlets were neither dead nor sleeping. It was only by contrast that they appeared comatose and moribund.

Indeed, the degree of gayety was quite startling. I was at once invited to "gatherings" which rejoiced in the paradoxical title of "Mum Sociables," where a penalty of five cents was imposed on each person for speaking (the revenue to go toward buying a new hearse, a cheerful object of benevolence), and the occasions were most enjoyable. There was also a "crazy party" at Way-back, the next village. This special form of lunacy I did not indulge in—farming was enough for me—but the painter who was enlivening my dining-room with a coating of vivid red and green, kindly told me all about it, how much I missed, and how the couple looked who took the first prize. The lady wore tin plates, tin cans, tin spoons, etc., sewed on to skirt and waist in fantastic patterns, making music as she walked, and on her head a battered old coffee pot, with artificial flowers which had outlived their usefulness sticking out of the spout; and her winning partner was arrayed in rag patchwork of the most demented variety.

"Youdorter gone" said he; "'twas a great show. But I bet youder beaten the hull lot on 'em if you'd set your mind on't!"

My walls were now covered with old-fashioned papers, five and ten cents a roll, and cheap matting improved the floors. But how to furnish eleven rooms? This brings me to—

CHAPTER II
AUCTIONS

"Going, going, gone."

Next came the excitement of auctions, great occasions, and of vital importance to me, as I was ambitious to furnish the entire house for one hundred dollars.

When the head of a family dies a settlement of the estate seems to make an auction necessary. I am glad of the custom, it proved of invaluable service to me, and the mortality among old people was quite phenomenal at Gooseville and thereabouts last year. While I deeply regretted the demise of each and all, still this general taking off was opportune for my needs.

There were seventeen auctions last season, and all but two were attended by me or my representatives.

A country auction is not so exciting as one in the city; still you must be wide-awake and cool, or you will be fleeced. An experienced friend, acquainted with the auctioneer, piloted me through my first sale, and for ten dollars I bought enough really valuable furniture to fill a large express wagon—as a large desk with drawers, little and big, fascinating pigeon holes, and a secret drawer, for two dollars; queer old table, ten cents; good solid chairs, nine cents each; mahogany center-table, one dollar and sixteen cents; and, best of all, a tall and venerable clock for the landing, only eight dollars! Its "innards" sadly demoralized, but capable of resuscitation, the weights being tin-cans filled with sand and attached by strong twine to the "works." It has to be wound twice daily, and when the hour hand points to six and the other to ten, I guess that it is about quarter past two, and in five minutes I hear the senile timepiece strike eleven!

The scene was unique. The sale had been advertised in post-office and stores as beginning at 10 A.M., but at eleven the farmers and their women folks were driving toward the house. A dozen old men, chewing tobacco and looking wise, were in the barn yard examining the stock to be sold, the carts and farming tools; a flock of hens were also to be disposed of, at forty cents each.

On such occasions the families from far and near who want to dispose of any old truck are allowed to bring it to add to the motley display. The really valuable possessions, if any, are kept back, either for private sale or to be divided among the heirs. I saw genuine antiques occasionally—old oak chests, finely carved oaken chairs—but these were rare. After the horses have been driven up and down the street, and with the other stock disposed of, it is time for lunch. Following the crowd into the kitchen, you see two barrels of crackers open, a mammoth cheese of the skim-milk species with a big knife by it, and on the stove a giant kettle in which cotton bags full of coffee are being distilled in boiling water. You are expected to dip a heavy white mug into the kettle for your share of the fragrant reviving beverage, cut off a hunk of cheese, and eat as many crackers as you can. It tasted well, that informal "free lunch."

Finding after one or two trials that the interested parties raised rapidly on anything I desired. I used to send Gusta and John, nicknamed very properly "Omniscience and Omnipotence," which names did equally well when reversed (like a paper cuff), and they, less verdant than their mistress, would return with an amazing array of stuff. We now have everything but a second-hand pulpit, a wooden leg, and a coffin plate. We utilized a cradle and antique churn as a composite flower stand; an immense spinning-wheel looks pretty covered with running vines, an old carriage lantern gleams brightly on my piazza every evening. I nearly bought a horse for fifteen dollars, and did secure a wagon for one dollar and a half, which, after a few needed repairs, costing only twenty-six dollars, was my pride, delight and comfort, and the envy of the neighborhood. Men came from near and far to examine that wagon, felt critically of every wheel, admired the shining coat of dark-green paint, and would always wind up with: "I vum, if that 'ere wagon ain't fine! Why, it's wuth fifty dollars, now, ef it's wuth a cent!" After a hard day's work, it seemed a gratification to them to come with lanterns to renew their critical survey, making a fine Rembrandtish study as they stood around it and wondered. A sleigh was bought for three dollars which, when painted by our home artist, is both comfortable and effective.

At one auction, where I was the only woman present, I bid on three shovels (needed to dig worms for my prize hens!) and, as the excitement increased with a rise in bids from two cents to ten, I cried, "Eleven!" And the gallant old fellow in command roared out as a man opened his mouth for "Twelve!": "I wouldn't bid ag'in a woman ef I'se you. Let 'er have 'em! Madam, Mum, or Miss—I can't pernounce your name and don't rightly know how to spell it—but the shovels are yourn!"

Attending auctions may be an acquired taste, but it grows on one like any other habit, and whenever a new and tempting announcement calls, I rise to the occasion and hasten to the scene of action, be the weather what it may. And many a treasure has been picked up in this way. Quaint old mirrors with the queerest pictures above, brass knockers, candlesticks of queer patterns, cups and saucers and plates, mugs of all sizes, from one generous enough to satisfy the capacities of a lager-soaked Dutchman to a dear little child's mug, evidently once belonging to a series. Mine was for March. A mother sitting on a bench, with a bowl of possibly Lenten soup by her side, is reproving a fat little fellow for his gross appetite at this solemn season. He is weeping, and on her other side a pet dog is pleading to be fed. The rhyme explains the reason:

> The jovial days of feasting past,
>
> 'Tis pious prudence come at last;
>
> And eager gluttony is taught
>
> To be content with what it ought.

A warming pan and a foot stove, just as it was brought home from a merry sleigh-ride, or a solemn hour at the "meetin'-house," recalling that line of Thomas Gray's:

> E'en in our ashes live their wonted fires.

Sometimes I would offer a little more to gain some coveted treasure already bid off. How a city friend enjoyed the confidences of a man who had agreed to sell for a profit! How he chuckled as he told of "one of them women who he guessed was a leetle crazy." "Why, jest think on't! I only paid ten cents for that hull lot on the table yonder, and *she*" (pointing to me) "*she* gin me a quarter for that old pair o' tongs!"

One day I heard some comments on myself after I had bid on a rag carpet and offered more than the other women knew it was worth.

"She's got a million, I hear."

"Wanter know—merried?"

"No; just an old maid."

"Judas Priest! Howd she git it?"

"Writin', I 'spoze. She writes love stories and sich for city papers. Some on 'em makes a lot."

It is not always cheering to overhear too much. When some of my friends, whom I had taken to a favorite junk shop, felt after two hours of purchase and exploration that they must not keep me waiting any longer, the man, in his eagerness to make a few more sales, exclaimed: "Let her wait; *her* time ain't wuth nothin'!"

At an auction last summer, one man told me of a very venerable lantern, an heirloom in his first wife's family, *so* long, measuring nearly a yard with his hands. I said I should like to go with him to see it, as I was making a collection of lanterns. He looked rather dazed, and as I turned away he inquired of my friend "if I wusn't *rather—*" She never allowed him to finish, and his lantern is now mine.

People seem to have but little sentiment about their associations with furniture long in the family.

The family and a few intimate friends usually sit at the upper windows gazing curiously on the crowd, with no evidence of feeling or pathetic recollections.

I lately heard a daughter say less than a month after her father's death, pointing to a small cretonne-covered lounge: "Father made me that lounge with his own hands when I's a little girl. He tho't a sight on't it, and allers kep' it 'round. But my house is full now. I ain't got no room for't." It sold for twelve cents!

Arthur Helps says that human nature craves, nay *enjoys*, tragedy; and when away from dramatic representation of crime and horrors and sudden death, as in this quiet country life, the people gratify their needs in the sorrows, sins, and calamities that befall their neighbors.

I strongly incline to Hawthorne's idea that furniture becomes magnetized, permeated, semi-vitalized, so that the chairs, sofas, and tables that have outlived their dear owners in my own family have almost a sacred value to me.

Still, why moralize. Estates must be settled, and auctions are a blessing in disguise.

Of course, buying so much by substitutes, I amassed a lot of curious things, of which I did not know the use or value, and therefore greatly enjoyed the experience of the Spectator as given in the Christian Union.

He attended an auction with the following result: "A long table was covered with china, earthenware, and glass; and the mantel beyond, a narrow shelf quite near the ceiling, glittered with a tangled maze of clean brass candlesticks, steel snuffers, and plated trays. At one end dangled a huge warming pan, and on the wall near it hung a bit of canvas in a gilded frame, from which the portrait had as utterly faded as he whom it represented had vanished into thin air. It was a strange place, a room from which many a colonial citizen had passed to take a stroll upon the village street; and here, in sad confusion to be sure, the dishes that graced his breakfast table. The Spectator could have lingered there if alone for half a day, but not willingly for half an hour in such a crowd. The crowd, however, closed every exit and he had to submit. A possible chance to secure some odd bit was his only consolation. Why the good old soul who last occupied the house, and who was born in it fourscore years ago, should necessarily have had only her grandmother's tableware, why every generation of this family should have suffered no losses by breakage, was not asked. Every bit, even to baking-powder prizes of green and greasy glass, antedated the Revolution, and the wise and mighty of Smalltown knew no better. A bit of egg shell sticking to a cracked teacup was stolen as a relic of Washington's last breakfast in Smalltown.

"While willow-pattern china was passing into other hands the Spectator made a discovery. A curious piece of polished, crooked mahogany was seen lying between soup tureens and gravy boats. He picked it up cautiously, fearing to attract attention, and, with one eye everywhere else, scanned it closely. What a curious paper-knife! he thought, and slyly tucked it back of a pile of plates. This must be kept track of; it may prove a veritable prize. But all his care went for naught. A curious old lady at his elbow had seen every action. 'What is it?' she asked, and the wooden wonder was brought to light. 'It's an old-fashioned wooden butter knife. I've seen 'em 'afore this. Don't you know in old times it wasn't everybody as had silver, and mahogany knives for butter was put on the table for big folks. We folks each used our own knife.' All this was dribbled into the Spectator's willing ears, and have the relic he would at any cost. Time and again he nervously turned it over to be sure that it was on the table, and so excited another's curiosity. 'What is it?' a second and still older lady asked. 'A colonial butter knife,' the Spectator replied with an air of much antiquarian lore. 'A butter knife! No such thing. My grandfather had one just like this, and it's a pruning knife. He wouldn't use a steel knife because it poisoned the sap.' What next? Paper knife, butter knife, and pruning knife! At all events every new name added a dollar to its value, and the Spectator wondered what the crowd would say, for now it was in the auctioneer's hands. He looked at it with a puzzled expression and merely cried: 'What is bid for *this*?' His ignorance was encouraging. It started at a dime and the Spectator secured it for a quarter. For a moment he little wondered at the fascination of public sales. The past was forgiven, for now luck had turned and he gloried in the possession of a prize.

"To seek the outer world was a perilous undertaking for fear that the triply-named knife might come to grief; but a snug harbor was reached at last, and hugging the precious bit, the Spectator mysteriously disappeared on reaching his home. No one must know of his success until the mystery was cleaned, brightened, and restored to pristine beauty. The Spectator rubbed the gummy surface with kerosene, and then polished it with flannel. Then warm water and a tooth brush were brought into play, and the oil all removed. Then a long dry polishing, and the restoration was complete. Certainly no other Smalltowner had such a wooden knife; and it was indeed beautiful. Black in a cross light, red in direct light, and kaleidoscopic by gaslight. Ah, such a prize! The family knew that something strange was transpiring, but what no one had an inkling. They must wait patiently, and they did. The Spectator proudly appeared, his prize in hand. 'See there!' he cried in triumph, and they all looked eagerly; and when the Spectator's pride was soaring at its highest, a younger daughter cried, 'Why, papa, it's the back of a hair-brush!' And it was."

An auctioneer usually tries to be off-hand, waggish, and brisk—a cross between a street peddler and a circus clown, with a hint of the forced mirth of the after-dinner speaker. Occasionally the jokes are good and the answers from the audience show the ready Yankee wit.

Once an exceedingly fat man, too obese to descend from his high wagon, bought an immense dinner bell and he was hit unmercifully. A rusty old fly-catcher elicited many remarks—as "no flies on that." I bought several chests, half full of rubbish, but found, alas! no hidden treasure, no missing jewels, no money hid away by miserly fingers and forgotten. Jake Corey, who was doing some work for me, encouraged me to hope. He said: "I hear ye patronize auctions putty reg'lar; sometimes there is a good deal to be made that way, and then ag'in there isn't. I never had no luck that way, but it's like getting married, it's a lottery! Folks git queer and put money in some spot, where they're apt to forget all about it. Now I knew a man who bought an old hat and a sight of other stuff; jest threw in the hat. And when he got home and come to examine it ef thar warn't three hundred dollars in good bills, chucked in under the sweater!"

"You ought to git over to Mason's auction to Milldon, sure. It's day after to-morrow at nine sharp. You see he'd a fortune left him, but he run straight through it buying the goldarndest things you ever heerd tell on—calves with six legs, dogs with three eyes or two tails, steers that could be druv most as well as hosses (Barnum he got hold o' 'em and tuk 'em round with his show); all sorts o' curious fowl and every outlandish critter he could lay his hands on. 'T stands to reason he couldn't run that rig many years. Your goin's on here made me think o' Mason. He cut a wide swath for a time.

"Wall, I hope you'll come off better'n he did. He sunk such a pile that he got discouraged and took to drink; then his wife, a mighty likely woman she is (one o' the Batchelders of Dull Corner), couldn't stand it and went back to her old home, and he died ragged and friendless about a month ago. Ef I's you, I'd go over, just to take warning and hold up in time."

CHAPTER III
BUYING A HORSE

"And you know this Deacon Elkins to be a thoroughly reliable man in every respect?"

"Indeed, I do," said honest Nathan Robbins. "He is the very soul of honor; couldn't do a mean thing. I'd trust him with all I have."

"Well, I'm glad to hear this, for I'm just going to buy a horse of him."

"A horse?"

"Yes—a horse!"

"Then I don't know anything about him!"

A TRUE TALE.

After furnishing my house in the aforesaid economical and nondescript fashion, came the trials of "planting time." This was such an unfragrant and expensive period that I pass over it as briefly as possible. I saw it was necessary in conformity with the appalling situation to alter one vowel in my Manorial Hall. The haul altogether amounted to eighteen loads besides a hundred bags of vilely smelling fertilizers. Agents for every kind of phosphates crowded around me, descanting on the needs of the old land, until I began to comprehend what the owner meant by "keeping it up." With Gail Hamilton, I had supposed the entire land of this earth to be pretty much the same age until I adopted the "abandoned." This I found was fairly senile in its worthless decrepitude.

My expenditure was something prodigious.

Yes, "planting time" was a nightmare in broad daylight, but as I look back, it seems a rosy dream, compared with the prolonged agonies of buying a horse!

All my friends said I must have a horse to truly enjoy the country, and it seemed a simple matter to procure an animal for my own use.

Livery-stable keepers, complaisant and cordial, were continually driving around the corner into my yard, with a tremendous flourish and style, chirking up old by-gones, drawing newly painted buggies, patched-up phaetons, two-seated second-hand "Democrats," high wagons, low chaises, just for me to try. They all said that seeing I was a lady and had just come among 'em, they would trade easy and treat me well. Each mentioned the *real* value, and a much lower price, at which I, as a special favor, could secure the entire rig. Their prices were all abominably exorbitant, so I decided to hire for a season. The dozen beasts tried in two months, if placed in a row, would cure the worst case of melancholia. Some shied; others were liable to be overcome by "blind staggers"; three had the epizootic badly, and longed to lie down; one was nearly blind. At last I was told of a lady who desired to leave her pet horse and Sargent buggy in some country home during her three months' trip abroad.

Both were so highly praised as *just the thing* that I took them on faith.

I judge that a woman can lie worse than a man about a horse!

"You will love my Nellie" she wrote. "I hate to part with her, even for the summer. She has been a famous racer in Canada—can travel easily twenty-five miles a day. Will go better at the end of the journey than at the beginning. I hear you are an accomplished driver, so I send my pet to your care without anxiety."

I sent a man to her home to drive out with this delightful treasure, and pictured myself taking long and daily drives over our excellent country roads. Nellie, *dear* Nellie; I loved her already. How I would pet her, and how fond she would become of me. Two lumps of sugar at least, every day for her, and red ribbons for the whip. How she would dash along! A horse for me at last! About 1.45 A.M., of the next day, a carriage was heard slowly entering the yard. I could hardly wait until morning to gloat over my gentle racer! At early dawn I visited the stable and found John disgusted beyond measure with my bargain. A worn-out, tumble-down, rickety carriage with wobbling wheels, and an equally worn-out, thin, dejected, venerable animal, with an immense blood spavin on left hind leg, recently blistered! It took three weeks of constant doctoring, investment in Kendall's Spavin Cure, and consultation with an expensive veterinary surgeon, to get the whilom race horse into a condition to slowly walk to market. I understood now the force of the one truthful clause—"She will go better at the end of the drive than at the beginning," for it was well-nigh impossible to get her stiff legs started without a fire kindled under them and a measure of oats held enticingly before her. It was enraging, but nothing to after experiences. All the disappointed livery men, their complaisance and cordiality, wholly a thing of the past, were jubilant that I had been so imposed upon by some one, even if they had failed. And their looks, as they wheeled rapidly by me, as I crept along with the poor, suffering, limping "Nellie," were almost more than I could endure.

Horses were again brought for inspection, and there was a repetition of previous horrors. At last a man came from Mossgrown. He had an honest face; he knew of a man who knew of a man whose brother had just *the* horse for me, "sound, stylish, kind, gentle as a lamb, fast as the wind." Profiting by experience, I said I would look at it. Next day, a young man, gawky and seemingly unsophisticated, brought the animal. It looked well enough, and I was so tired. He was anxious to sell, but only because he was going to be married and go West; needed money. And he said with sweet simplicity: "Now I ain't no jockey, I ain't! You needn't be afeard of me—I say just what I mean. I want spot cash, I do, and you can have horse, carriage, and harness for $125 down." He gave me a short drive, and we did go "like the wind." I thought the steed very hard to hold in, but he convinced me that it was not so. I decided to take the creature a week on trial, which was a blow to that guileless young man. And that very afternoon I started for the long, pleasant drive I had been dreaming about since early spring.

The horse looked quiet enough, but I concluded to take my German domestic along for extra safety. I remembered his drawling direction, "Doan't pull up the reins unless you want him to go pretty lively," so held the reins rather loosely for a moment only, for this last hope wheeled round the corner as if possessed, and after trotting, then breaking, then darting madly from side to side, started into a full run. I pulled with all my might; Gusta stood up and helped. No avail. On we rushed to sudden death. No one in sight anywhere. With one

Herculean effort, bred of the wildest despair, we managed to rein him in at a sharp right angle, and we succeeded in calming his fury, and tied the panting, trembling fiend to a post. Then Gusta mounted guard while I walked home in the heat and dirt, fully half a mile to summon John.

I learned that *that* horse had never before been driven by a woman. He evidently was not pleased.

Soon the following appeared among the local items of interest in the Gooseville Clarion:

Uriel Snooks, who has been working in the cheese factory at Frogville, is now to preside over chair number four in Baldwin's Tonsorial Establishment on Main Street.

Kate Sanborn is trying another horse.

These bits of information in the papers were a boon to the various reporters, but most annoying to me. The Bungtown Gazetteer announced that "a well-known Boston poetess had purchased the Britton Farm, and was fitting up the old homestead for city boarders!" I couldn't import a few hens, invest in a new dog, or order a lawn mower, but a full account would grace the next issue of all the weeklies. I sympathized with the old woman who exclaimed in desperation:

"Great Jerusalem, ca'nt I stir,

Without a-raisin' some feller's fur?"

At last I suspected the itinerant butcher of doing double duty as a reporter, and found that he "was engaged by several editors to pick up bits of news for the press" as he went his daily rounds. "But this," I exclaimed, "is just what I don't want and can't allow. Now if you should drive in here some day and discover me dead, reclining against yonder noble elm, or stark at its base, surrounded by my various pets, don't allude to it in the most indirect way. I prefer the funeral to be strictly private. Moreover, if I notice another 'item' about me, I'll buy of your rival." And the trouble ceased.

But the horses! Still they came and went. I used to pay my friend the rubicund surgeon to test some of these highly recommended animals in a short drive with me.

One pronounced absolutely unrivaled was discovered by my wise mentor to be "watch-eyed," "rat-tailed," with a swollen gland on the neck, would shy at a stone, stand on hind legs for a train, with various other minor defects. I grew fainthearted, discouraged, cynical, bitter. Was there no horse for me? I became town-talk as "a dreful fussy old maid who didn't know her own mind, and couldn't be suited *no* way."

I remember one horse brought by a butcher from West Bungtown. It was, in the vernacular, a buck-skin. Hide-bound, with ribs so prominent they suggested a wash-board. The two fore legs were well bent out at the knees; both hind legs were swelled near the hoofs. His ears nearly as large as a donkey's; one eye covered with a cataract, the other deeply sunken. A Roman nose, accentuated by a wide stripe, aided the pensive expression of his drooping under lip. He leaned against the shafts as if he were tired.

"There, Marm," said the owner, eying my face as an amused expression stole over it; "ef you don't care for *style*, ef ye want a good, steddy critter, and a critter that can *go*, and a critter that *any* lady can drive, *there's* the critter for ye!"

I did buy at last, for life had become a burden. An *interested* neighbor (who really pitied me?) induced me to buy a pretty little black horse. I named him "O.K."

After a week I changed to "N.G."

After he had run away, and no one would buy him, "D.B."

At last I succeeded in exchanging this shying and dangerous creature for a melancholy, overworked mare at a livery stable. I hear that "D.B." has since killed two *I*-talians by throwing them out when not sufficiently inebriated to fall against rocks with safety.

And my latest venture is a *backer*.

Horses have just as many disagreeable traits, just as much individuality in their badness, as human beings. Under kind treatment, daily petting, and generous feeding, "Dolly" is too frisky and headstrong for a lady to drive.

"Sell that treacherous beast at once or you will be killed," writes an anxious friend who had a slight acquaintance with her moods.

I want now to find an equine reliance whose motto is "Nulla vestigia retrorsum," or "No steps backward."

I have pasted Mr. Hale's famous motto, "Look forward and not back," over her stall—but with no effect. The "Lend a Hand" applies to those we yell for when the backing is going on.

By the way, a witty woman said the other day that men always had the advantage. A woman looked back and was turned into a pillar of salt; Bellamy looked back and made sixty thousand dollars.

Mr. Robert B. Roosevelt, in his amusing book "Five Acres too Much" gives even a more tragic picture, saying: "My experience of horseflesh has been various and instructive. I have been thrown over their heads and slid over their tails; have been dragged by saddle, stirrups, and tossed out of wagons. I have had them to back and to kick, to run and to bolt, to stand on their hind feet and kick with their front, and then reciprocate by standing on their front and kicking with their hind feet.... I have been thrown much with horses and more by them."

"Horses are the most miserable creatures, invariably doing precisely what they ought not to do; a pest, a nuisance, a bore." Or, as some one else puts it:

"A horse at its best is an amiable idiot; at its worst, a dangerous maniac."

CHAPTER IV
FOR THOSE WHO LOVE PETS

"All were loved and all were regretted, but life is made up of forgetting."

"The best thing which a man possesses is his dog."

When I saw a man driving into my yard after this, I would dart out of a back door and flee to sweet communion with my cows.

On one such occasion I shouted back that I did not want a horse of any variety, could not engage any fruit trees, did not want the place photographed, and was just going out to spend the day. I was courteously but firmly informed that my latest visitor had, singular to relate, no horse to dispose of, but he "would like fourteen dollars for my dog tax for the current year!" As he was also sheriff, constable, and justice of the peace, I did not think it worth while to argue the question, although I had no more thought of being called up to pay a dog tax than a hen tax or cat tax. I trembled, lest I should be obliged to enumerate my entire menagerie—cats, dogs, canaries, rabbits, pigs, ducks, geese, hens, turkeys, pigeons, peacocks, cows, and horses.

Each kind deserves an entire chapter, and how easy it would be to write of cats and their admirers from Cambyses to Warner; of dogs and their friends from Ulysses to Bismarck. I agree with Ik Marvel that a cat is like a politician, sly and diplomatic; purring—for food; and affectionate—for a consideration; really caring nothing for friendship and devotion, except as means to an end. Those who write books and articles and verse and prose tributes to cats think very differently, but the cats I have met have been of this type.

And dogs. Are they really so affectionate, or are they also a little shrewd in licking the hand that feeds them? I dislike to be pessimistic. But when my dogs come bounding to meet me for a jolly morning greeting they do seem expectant and hungry rather than affectionate. At other hours of the day they plead with loving eyes and wagging tails for a walk or a seat in the carriage or permission to follow the wagon.

But I will not analyze their motives. They fill the house and grounds with life and frolic, and a farm would be incomplete if they were missing. Hamerton, in speaking of the one dog, the special pet and dear companion of one's youth, observes that "the comparative shortness of the lives of dogs is the only imperfection in the relation between them and us. If they had lived to three-score and ten, man and dog might have traveled through life together, but, as it is, we must either have a succession of affections, or else, when the first is buried in its early grave, live in a chill condition of dog-less-ness."

I thank him for that expressive compound word. Almost every one might, like Grace Greenwood and Gautier, write a History of my Pets and make a readable book. Carlyle, the grand old growler, was actually attached to a little white dog—his wife's special delight, for whom she used to write cute little notes to the master. And when he met with a fatal accident, he was tenderly nursed by both for months, and when the doctor was at last obliged to put him out of pain by prussic acid, their grief was sincere. They buried him at the top of the garden in Cheyne Row, and planted cowslips round his grave, and his mistress placed a stone tablet, with name and date, to mark the last resting place of her blessed dog.

"I could not have believed," writes Carlyle in the Memorials, "my grief then and since would have been the twentieth part of what it was—nay, that the want of him would have been to me other than a riddance. Our last midnight walk together (for he insisted on trying to come), January 31st, is still painful to my thought. Little dim, white speck of life, of love, of fidelity, girdled by the darkness of night eternal."

Beecher said many a good thing about dogs, but I like this best: Speaking of horseback riding, he incidentally remarked that in evolution, the human door was just shut upon the horse, but the dog got fully up before the door was shut. If there was not reason, mirthfulness, love, honor, and fidelity in a dog, he did not know where to look for it. Oh, if they only could speak, what wise and humorous and sarcastic things they would say! Did you never feel snubbed by an immense dog you had tried to patronize? And I have seen many a dog smile. Bayard Taylor says: "I know of nothing more moving, indeed semi-tragic, than the yearning helplessness in the face of a dog, who understands what is said to him, and can not answer!"

Dr. Holland wrote a poem to his dog Blanco, "his dear, dumb friend," in which he expresses what we all have felt many times.

I look into your great brown eyes,
   Where love and loyal homage shine,
And wonder where the difference lies
   Between your soul and mine.

The whole poem is one of the best things Holland ever did in rhyme. He was ambitious to be remembered as a poet, but he never excelled in verse unless he had something to express that was very near his heart. He was emphatically the Apostle of Common Sense. How beautifully he closes his loving tribute—

Ah, Blanco, did I worship God
   As truly as you worship me,
Or follow where my Master trod
   With your humility,

Did I sit fondly at his feet
   As you, dear Blanco, sit at mine,
And watch him with a love as sweet,
   My life would grow divine!

Almost all our great men have more than one dog in their homes. When I spent a day with the Quaker poet at Danvers, I found he had three dogs. Roger Williams, a fine Newfoundland, stood on the piazza with the questioning, patronizing air of a dignified host; a bright-faced Scotch terrier, Charles Dickens, peered at us from the window, as if glad of a little excitement; while Carl, the graceful greyhound, was indolently coiled up on a shawl and took little notice of us.

Whittier has also a pet cow, favorite and favored, which puts up her handsome head for an expected caress. The kindly hearted old poet, so full of tenderness for all created things, told me that years when nuts were scarce he would put beech nuts and acorns here and there as he walked over his farm, to cheer the squirrels by an unexpected find.

Miss Mitford's tribute to her defunct doggie shows to what a degree of imbecility an old maid may carry fondness for her pets, but it is pathetically amusing.

"My own darling Mossy's hair, cut off after he was dead by dear Drum, August 22, 1819. He was the greatest darling that ever lived (son of Maria and Mr. Webb's 'Ruler,' a famous dog given him by Lord Rivers), and was, when he died, about seven or eight years old. He was a large black dog, of the largest and strongest kind of greyhounds; very fast and honest, and resolute past example; an excellent killer of hares, and a most magnificent and noble-looking creature. His coat was of the finest and most glossy black, with no white, except a very little under his feet (pretty white shoe linings I used to call them)—a little beautiful white spot, quite small, in the very middle of his neck, between his chin and his breast—and a white mark on his bosom. His face was singularly beautiful; the finest black eyes, very bright, and yet sweet, and fond, and tender—eyes that seemed to speak; a beautiful, complacent mouth, which used sometimes to show one of the long white teeth at the side; a jet black nose; a brow which was bent and flexible, like Mr. Fox's, and gave great sweetness and expression, and a look of thought to his dear face. There never was such a dog! His temper was, beyond comparison, the sweetest ever known. Nobody ever saw him out of humor. And his sagacity was equal to his temper. Thank God, he went off without suffering. He must have died in a moment. I thought I should have broken my heart when I came home and found what had happened. I shall miss him every moment of my life; I have missed him every instant to-day—so have Drum and Granny. He was laid out last night in the stable, and this morning we buried him in the middle plantation on the house side of the fence, in the flowery corner, between the fence and Lord Shrewsbury's fields. We covered his dear body with flowers; every flower in the garden. *Everybody loved him*; 'dear saint,' as I used to call him, and as *I do not doubt he now is!!* No human being was ever so faithful, so gentle, so generous, and so fond! I shall never love anything half so well.

"It will always be pleasant to me to remember that I never teased him by petting other things, and that everything I had he shared. He always ate half my breakfast, and the very day before he died I fed him *all the morning* with filberts." (There may have been a connection between the filberts and the funeral.)

"While I had him, I was always sure of having one who would love me alike in riches or poverty, who always looked at me with looks of the fondest love, always faithful and always kind. To think of him was a talisman against vexing thoughts. A thousand times I have said, 'I want my Mossy,' when that dear Mossy was close by and would put his dear black nose under my hand on hearing his name. God bless you, my Mossy! I cried when you died, and I can hardly help crying whenever I think of you. All who loved me loved Mossy. He had the most perfect confidence in me—always came to me for protection against any one who threatened him, and, thank God, always found it. I value all things he had lately or ever touched; even the old quilt that used to be spread on my bed for him to lie on, and which we called Mossy's quilt; and the pan that he used to drink out of in the parlor, and which was always called Mossy's pan, dear darling!

"I forgot to say that his breath was always sweet and balmy; his coat always glossy like satin; and he never had any disease or anything to make him disagreeable in his life. Many other things I have omitted; and so I should if I were to write a whole volume of his praise; for he was above all praise, sweet angel! I have inclosed some of his hair, cut off by papa after his death, and some of the hay on which he was laid out. He died Saturday, the 21st of August, 1819, at Bertram House. Heaven bless him, beloved angel!"

It is as sad as true that great natures are solitary, and therefore doubly value the affections of their pets.

Southey wrote a most interesting biography of the cats of Greta Hall, and on the demise of one wrote to an old friend: "Alas! Grosvenor, this day poor old Rumpel was found dead, after as long and as happy a life as cat could wish for—if cats form wishes on that subject. There should be a court mourning in Cat-land, and if the Dragon wear a black ribbon round his neck, or a band of crape, *à la militaire*, round one of the fore paws, it will be but a becoming mark of respect. As we have not catacombs here, he is to be decently interred in the orchard and catnip planted on his grave."

And so closes this catalogue of Southey's "Cattery."

But, hark! my cats are mewing, dogs all calling for me—no—for dinner! After all, what is the highest civilization but a thin veneer over natural appetites? What would a club be without its *chefs*, a social affair without refreshment, a man without his dinner, a woman without her tea? Come to think of it, I'm hungry myself!

CHAPTER V
STARTING A POULTRY FARM

If every hen should only raise five broods yearly of ten each, and there were ten hens to start with, at the end of two years they would number 344,760, after the superfluous roosters were sold; and then, supposing the extra eggs to have paid for their keeping and the produce to be worth only a dollar and a half a pair, there would be a clear profit of $258,520. Allowing for occasional deaths, this sum might be stated in round numbers at a quarter of a million, which would be a liberal increase from ten hens. Of course I did not expect to do as well as this, but merely mention what might be done with good luck and forcing.

ROBERT ROOSEVELT.

Having always heard, on the best authority, that there was "money in hens," I invested largely in prize fowls secured at State fairs and large poultry shows, buying as many kinds as possible to make an effective and brilliant display in their "runs."

There *is* a good deal of money in my hens—how to get it back is the present problem. These hens were all heralded as famous layers; several did lay in the traveling coops on the journey, great pinky-brown beauties, just to show what they could do if they chose, then stopped suddenly. I wrote anxiously to former owners of this vaunted stock to explain such disappointing behavior. Some guessed the hens were just moulting, others thought "may be they were broody"; a few had the frankness to agree with me that it was mighty curious, but hens always were "sorter contrary critters."

Their appetites remained normal, but, as the little girl said of her pet bantam, they only lay about doing nothing. And when guests desired some of my fine fresh eggs boiled for breakfast, I used to go secretly to a neighbor and buy a dozen, but never gave away the mortifying situation.

Seeing piles of ducks' eggs in a farmer's barn, all packed for market, and picturing the producers, thirty white Pekins, a snowy, self-supporting fleet on my reformed lakelet, I bought the whole lot, and for long weary months they were fed and pampered and coaxed and reasoned with, shut up, let out, kept on the water, forbidden to go to it, but not one egg to be seen!

It was considered a rich joke in that locality that a city woman who was trying to farm, had applied for these ducks just as they had completed their labors for the season of 1888-'90; they were also extremely venerable, and the reticent owner rejoiced to be relieved of an expensive burden at good rates. Knowing nothing of these facts in natural history, I pondered deeply over the double phenomenon. I said the hens seemed normal only as to appetite; the ducks proved abnormal in this respect. They were always coming up to the back door, clamoring for food—always unappeased. They preferred cake, fresh bread, hot boiled potatoes, doted on tender bits of meat, but would gobble up anything and everything, more voracious and less fastidious than the ordinary hog of commerce. Bags of corn were consumed in a flash, "shorts" were never long before their eager gaze, they went for every kind of nourishment provided for the rest of the menagerie. A goat is supposed to have a champion appetite and digestion, but a duck—at least one of my ducks—leaves a goat so far behind that he never could regain his reputation for omniverosity. They were too antique to be eaten themselves—their longevity entitled them to respect; they could not be disposed of by the shrewdest market man to the least particular of boarding-house providers; I could only regard them with amazement and horror and let them go on eating me out of house and home and purse-strings.

But at last I knew. I asked an honest man from afar, who called to sell something, why those ducks would not lay a single egg. He looked at them critically and wrote to me the next day:

"DEAR MADAM: The reason your ducks won't lay is because they're too old to live and the biggest part of 'em is drakes.

Respectfully,

JONAS HURLBERT."

I hear that there are more ducks in the Chinese Empire than in all the world outside of it. They are kept by the Celestials on every farm, on the private and public roads, on streets of cities, and on all the lakes, ponds, rivers, streams, and brooks in the country. That is the secret of their lack of progress. What time have they to advance after the ducks are fed and cared for? No male inhabitant could ever squeeze out a leisure half-hour to visit a barber, hence their long queues.

About this time the statement of Mr. Crankin, of North Yeaston, Rhode Island, that he makes a clear and easy profit of five dollars and twenty cents per hen each year, and nearly forty-four dollars to every duck, and might have increased said profit if he had hatched, rather than sold, seventy-two dozen eggs, struck me as wildly apocryphal. Also that caring for said hens and ducks was merely an incident of his day's work on the large farm, he working with his laborers. Heart-sick and indignant, contrasting his rosy success with my leaden-hued failure, I decided to give all my ducks away, as they wouldn't, couldn't drown, and there would be no use in killing them. But no one wanted them! And everybody smiled quizzically when I proposed the gift.

Just then, as if in direct sarcasm, a friend sent me a paper with an item marked to the effect that a poor young girl had three ducks' eggs given her as the basis of a solid fortune, and actually cleared one hundred and eighteen dollars from those three eggs the first year.

Another woman solemnly asserts in print a profit of $448.69 from one hundred hens each year.

The census man told me of a woman who had only eighteen hens. They gave her sixteen hundred and ninety eggs, of which she sold eighteen dollars' worth, leaving plenty for household use.

And my hens and my ducks! In my despair I drove a long way to consult a "duck man." He looked like the typical Brother Jonathan, only with a longer beard, and his face was haggard, unkempt, anxious. He could scarcely stop to converse, evidently grudged the time, devotes his entire energies from dawn to twilight to slaving for his eight hundred ducklings. He also kept an incubator going all the time.

"Do ducks pay you?" I asked.

"Wall, I'm gettin' to be somewhat of a bigotist," he said; "I barely git a livin'."

"Why Mr. Crankin—" I began.

The name roused his jealous ire, and his voice, a low mumble before, now burst into a loud roar. "Yes, Crankin makes money, has a sight o' incubators, makes 'em himself, sells a lot, but some say they don't act like his do when they git off his place; most on 'em seem possessed, but Crankin, *he* can manage 'em and makes money too."

"Do your ducks lay much?"

"Lay! I don't want 'em to lay! Sell 'em all out at nine weeks, 'fore the pin feathers come; then they're good eatin'—for them as likes 'em. I've heard of yure old lot. Kill 'em, I say, and start new!"

"Crankin says—"

"I don't care nothing what Crankin says" (here the voice would have filled a cathedral), "I tell ye; me and Crankin's two different critters!"

So I felt; but it would not do to give up. I purchased an expensive incubator and brooder—needn't have bought a brooder. I put into the incubator at a time when eggs were scarce and high priced, two hundred eggs—hens' eggs, ducks' eggs, goose eggs. The temperature must be kept from 102° to 104°. The lamps blazed up a little on the first day, but after that we kept the heat exactly right by daily watching and night vigils. It engrossed most of the time of four able-bodied victims.

Nothing ever was developed. The eggs were probably cooked that first day!

Now I'm vainly seeking for a purchaser for my I. and B. Terms of sale very reasonable. Great reduction from original price; shall no doubt be forced to give them away to banish painful recollections.

I also invested in turkeys, geese, and peacocks, and a pair of guinea hens to keep hawks away.

For long weary months the geese seemed the only fowls truly at home on my farm. They did their level best. Satisfied that my hens would neither lay nor set, I sent to noted poultry fanciers for "settings" of eggs at three dollars per thirteen, then paid a friendly "hen woman" for assisting in the mysterious evolution of said eggs into various interesting little families old enough to be brought to me.

Many and curious were the casualties befalling these young broods. Chickens are subject to all the infantile diseases of children and many more of their own, and mine were truly afflicted. *Imprimis*, most would not hatch; the finest Brahma eggs contained the commonest barn-yard fowls. Some stuck to the shell, some were drowned in a saucer of milk, some perished because no lard had been rubbed on their heads, others passed away discouraged by too much lard. Several ate rose bugs with fatal results; others were greedy as to gravel and agonized with distended crops till released by death. They had more "sand" than was good for them. They were raised on "Cat Hill," and five were captured by felines, and when the remnant was brought to me they disappeared day by day in the most puzzling manner until we caught our mischievous pug, "Tiny Tim," holding down a beautiful young Leghorn with his cruel paw and biting a piece out of her neck.

So they left me, one by one, like the illusions of youth, until there was no "survival of the fittest."

In a ragged old barn opposite, a hen had stolen her nest and brought out seventeen vigorous chicks. I paid a large bill for the care of what might have been a splendid collection, and meekly bought that faithful old hen with her large family. It is now a wonder to me that any chickens arrive at maturity. Fowls are afflicted with parasitic wrigglers in their poor little throats. The disease is called "gapes," because they try to open their bills for more air until a red worm in the trachea causes suffocation. This horrid red worm, called scientifically *Scelorostoma syngamus*, destroys annually *half a million* of chickens.

Dr. Crisp, of England, says it would be of truly national importance to find the means of preventing its invasion.

The unpleasant results of hens and garden contiguous, Warner has described. They are incompatible if not antagonistic. One man wisely advises: "Fence the garden in and let the chickens run, as the man divided the house with his quarrelsome wife, by taking the inside himself and giving her the outside, that she might have room according to her strength."

Looking over the long list of diseases to which fowls are subject is dispiriting. I am glad they can't read them, or they would have all at once, as J.K. Jerome, the witty playwright, decided he had every disease found in a medical dictionary, except housemaid's knee. Look at this condensed list:

DISEASES OF NERVOUS SYSTEM.—1. Apoplexy. 2. Paralysis. 3. Vertigo. 4. Neuralgia. 5. Debility.

DISEASES OF DIGESTIVE ORGANS.—99.

DISEASES OF LOCOMOTIVE ORGANS.—1. Rheumatism. 2. Cramp. 3. Gout. 4. Leg weakness. 5. Paralysis of legs. 6. Elephantiasis.

Next, diseases caused by parasites.

Then, injuries.

Lastly, miscellaneous.

I could add a still longer list of unclassified ills: Homesickness, fits, melancholia, corns, blindness from fighting too much, etc.

Now that I have learned to raise chickens, it is a hard and slow struggle to get any killed. I say in an off-hand manner, with assumed nonchalance: "Ellen, I want Tom to kill a rooster at once for tomorrow's dinner, and I have an order from a friend for four more, so he must select five to-night." Then begins the trouble. "Oh," pleads Ellen, "don't kill dear Dick! poor, dear Dick! That is Tom's pet of all; so big and handsome and knows so much! He will jump up on Tom's shoulder and eat out of his hand and come when he calls—and those big Brahmas—don't you know how they were brought up by hand, as you might say, and they know me and hang around the door for crumbs, and that beauty of a Wyandock, you *couldn't* eat *him!*" When the matter is decided, as the guillotining is going on, Ellen and I sit listening to the axe thuds and the death squaks, while she wrings her hands, saying: "O dearie me! What a world—the dear Lord ha' mercy on us poor creatures! What a thing to look into, that we must kill the poor innocents to eat them. And they were so tame and cunning, and would follow me all around!" Then I tell her of the horrors of the

French Revolution to distract her attention from the present crisis, and alluded to the horrors of cannibalism recently disclosed in Africa. Then I fall into a queer reverie and imagine how awful it would be if we should ever be called to submit to a race of beings as much larger than we are as we are above the fowls. I almost hear such a monster of a house-wife, fully ninety feet high, say to a servant, looking sternly and critically at me:

"That fat, white creature must be killed; just eats her old head off—will soon be too tough"—Ugh! Here Tom comes with five headless fowls. Wasn't that a weird fancy of mine?

Truly "Me and Crankin's two different critters."

From the following verse, quoted from a recent poultry magazine, I conclude that I must be classed as a "chump." As it contains the secret of success in every undertaking, it should be committed to memory by all my readers.

"Grit makes the man,

The want of it the chump.

The men who win,

Lay hold, hang on, and hump."

CHAPTER VI
GHOSTS

"But stop," says the courteous and prudent reader, "are there any such things as ghosts?"

"Any ghostesses!" cries Superstition, who settled long since in the country, near a church yard on a "rising ground," "any ghostesses! Ay, man, lots on 'em! Bushels on 'em! Sights on 'em! Why, there's one as walks in our parish, reglar as the clock strikes twelve—and always the same round, over church-stile, round the corner, through the gap, into Shorts Spinney, and so along into our close, where he takes a drink at the pump—for ye see he died in liquor, and then arter he squenched hisself, wanishes into waper.

"Then there's the ghost of old Beales, as goes o' nights and sows tares in his neighbor's wheat—I've often seed 'em in seed time. They do say that Black Ben, the poacher, have riz, and what's more, walked slap through all the squire's steel traps, without springing on 'em. And then there's Bet Hawkey as murdered her own infant—only the poor little babby hadn't learned to walk, and so can't appear ag'in her."

THOMAS HOOD, *The Grimsby Ghost*.

That dark little room I described as so convenient during a terrific thunderstorm or the prowling investigations of a burglar, began after a while to get mysterious and uncanny, and I disliked, nay, dreaded to enter it after dark. It was so still, so black, so empty, so chilly with a sort of supernatural chill, so silent, that imagination conjured up sounds such as I had never heard before. I had been told of an extremely old woman, a great-great-grandmother, bed-ridden, peevish, and weak-minded, who had occupied that room for nearly a score of years, apparently forgotten by fate, and left to drag out a monotonous, weary existence on not her "mattress grave" (like the poet Heine), but on an immensely thick feather bed; only a care, a burden, to her relations.

As twilight came on, I always carefully closed that door and shut the old lady in to sleep by herself. For it seemed that she was still there, still propped up in an imaginary bed, mumbling incoherently of the past, or moaning out some want, or calling for some one to bring a light, as she used to.

Once in a while, they told me, she would regain her strength suddenly and astonish the family by appearing at the door. When the grand-daughter was enjoying a Sunday night call from her "intended" it was rather embarrassing.

I said nothing to my friends about this unpleasant room. But several were susceptible to the strange influence. One thought she should not mind so much if the door swung open, and a *portière* concealed the gloom. So a cheerful cretonne soon was hung. Then the fancy came that the curtain stirred and swayed as if some one or something was groping feebly with ghostly or ghastly fingers behind it. And one night, when sitting late and alone over the embers of my open fire, feeling a little forlorn, I certainly heard moans coming from that direction.

It was not the wind, for, although it was late October and the breezes were sighing over summer's departure, this sound was entirely different and distinct. Then (and what a shiver ran down my back!) I remembered hearing that a woman had been killed by falling down the steep cellar stairs, and the spot on the left side where she was found unconscious and bleeding had been pointed out to me. There, I heard it again! Was it the wraith of the aged dame or the cries of that unfortunate creature? Hush! Ellen can't have fallen down!

I am really scared; the lamp seems to be burning dim and the last coal has gone out. Is it some restless spirit, so unhappy that it must moan out its weary plaint? I ought to be brave and go at once and look boldly down the cellar stairs and draw aside that waving *portière*. Oh, dear! If I only had some one to go with me and hold a light and—there it is—the third time. Courage vanished. It might be some dreadful tramp hiding and trying to drive me up-stairs, so he could get the silver, and he would gladly murder me for ten cents—

"Tom," I cried. "Tom, come here." But Tom, my six-footer factotum, made no response.

I could stand it no longer—the *portière* seemed fairly alive, and I rushed out to the kitchen where Ellen sat reading the *Ledger*, deep in the horrors of The Forsaken Inn. "Ellen, I'm ashamed, but I'm really frightened. I do believe somebody is in that horrid dark room, or in the cellar, and where *is* Tom?

"Bedad, Miss, and you've frightened the heart right out o' me. It might be a ghost, for there are such things (Heaven help us!), and I've seen 'em in this country and in dear old Ireland, and so has Tom."

"You've seen ghosts?"

"Yes, indeed, Miss, but I've never spoke to any, for you've no right to speak to a ghost, and if you do you will surely die." Tom now came in and soon satisfied me that there was no living thing in the darkness, so I sat down and listened to Ellen's experiences with ghosts.

THE FORMER MRS. WILKES.—"Now this happened in New York city, Miss, in West 28th Street, and is every word true, for, my dear, I saw it with my own eyes. I went to bed, about half-past nine it was this night, and I was lying quietly in bed, looking up to the ceiling; no light on account of the mosquitoes, and Maud, the little girl I was caring for, a romping dear of seven or eight, a motherless child, had been tossing about restless like, and her arm was flung over me. All at once I saw a lady standing by the side of the bed in her night dress and looking earnestly at the child beyond me. She then came nearer, took Maud's arm off me, and gently straightened her in bed, then stroked her face, both cheeks—fondly, you know—and then stood and looked at the child. I said not a word, but I wasn't one bit afraid for I thought it was a living lady. I could tell the color of her eyes and hair and just how she looked every way. In the morning I described her to Mrs. Wilkes, and asked, 'Is there any strange lady in the house?' 'No, Ellen. Why?' she said. Then I said: 'Why, there certainly was a pleasant-looking lady in my room last night, in her night dress, and she patted Maud as if she thought a sight of her.'

"'Why,' said my mistress, 'that is surely the former Mrs. Wilkes!'

"She said that the older daughter had seen her several times standing before her glass, fixing her hair and looking at herself, but if she spoke to her or tried to speak, her mother would take up something and shake it at her. And once when we were going up-stairs together Alice screamed, and said that her mother was at the top of the stairs and blew her cold breath right down on her. The stepmother started to give her her slipper, but the father pitied her and would not allow her to be whipped, and said 'I'll go up to bed with you, Alice.'"

"Did you ever see the lady in white again, Ellen?"

"Never, Ma'am, nor did I ever see any other ghost in this country that I was sure was a ghost, but—Ireland, dear old Ireland, oh, that's an ancient land, and they have both ghosts and fairies and banshees too, and many's the story I've heard over there, and from my own dear mother's lips, and she would not tell a lie (Heaven rest her soul!), and I've seen them myself over there, and so has Tom and his brother too, Miss. Oh, many's the story I could tell!"

"Well, Ellen, let me have one of your own—your very best." And I went for pencil and pad.

"And are ye going to pin down my story. Well, Miss, if ye take it just as I say, and then fix it proper to be read, they'll like it, for people are crazy now to get the true ghost stories of dear old Ireland. O Miss, when you go over, don't forget my native place. It has a real castle and a part of it is haunted, and the master doesn't like to live there—only comes once a year or so, for hunting—and the rabbits there are as thick as they can be and the river chuck full of fish, but no one can touch any game, or even take out one fish, or they would be punished."

"Yes, Ellen it's hard, and all wrong, but we are wandering away from your ghosts, and you know I am going to take notes. So begin."

"Well, Miss, I was a sort of companion or maid to a blind lady in my own town. I slept in a little room just across the landing from hers, so as to always be within reach of her. I was just going to bed, when she called for me to come in and see if there was something in the room—something alive, she thought, that had been hopping, hopping all around her bed, and frightened her dreadfully, poor thing, for, you remember, she was stone blind, Miss, which made it worse. So I hurried in and I shook the curtains, looked behind the bureau and under the bed, and tried everywhere for whatever might be hopping around, but could find nothing and heard not a sound. While I was there all was still. Then I went into my room again, and left the door open, as I thought Miss Lacy would feel more comfortable about it, and I was hardly in my bed when she called again and screamed out with fear, for It was hopping round the bed. She said I must go downstairs and bring a candle. So I had to go down-stairs to the pantry all alone and get the candle. Then I searched as before, but found nothing—not a thing. Well, my dear, I went into my room and kept my candle lighted this time. The third time she called me she was standing on her pillow, shivering with fright, and begged me to bring the light. It was sad, because she was stone blind. She told me how It went hopping around the room, with its legs tied like. And after looking once more and finding nothing, she said I'd have to sleep in the bed with her and bring a chair near the bed and put the lighted candle on it. For a long time we kept awake, and watched and listened, but nothing happened, nothing appeared. We kept awake as long as we could, but at last our eyes grew very heavy, and the lady seemed to feel more easy. So I snuffed out the candle. Out It hopped and kept a jumping on one leg like from one side to the other. We were so much afraid we covered our faces; we dreaded to see It, so we hid our eyes under the sheet, and she clung on to me all shaking; she felt worse because she was blind.

"We fell asleep at daylight, and when I told Monk, the butler, he said it was a corpse, sure—a corpse whose legs had been tied to keep them straight and the cords had not been taken off, the feet not being loosened. Why my own dear mother, that's dead many a year (Heaven bless her departed spirit!)—she would never tell a word that was not true—she saw a ghost hopping in that way, tied-like, jumping around a bed—blue as a blue bag; just after the third day she was buried, and my mother (the Lord bless her soul!) told me the sons went to her grave and loosened the cords and she never came back any more. Isn't it awful? And, bedad, Miss, it's every word true. I can tell you of a young man I knew who looked into a window at midnight (after he had been playing cards, Miss, gambling with the other boys) and saw something awful strange, and was turned by ghosts into a *shadow*."

This seemed to be a thrilling theme, such as Hawthorne would have been able to weave into the weirdest of weird tales, and I said, "Go on."

"Well, he used to go playing cards about three miles from his home with a lot of young men, for his mother wouldn't have cards played in her house, and she thought it was wicked, and begged him not to play. It's a habit with the young men of Ireland—don't know as it's the same in other countries—and they play for a goose or a chicken. They go to some vacant house to get away from their fathers, they're so against it at home. Why, my brother-in-law used to go often to such a house on the side of a country road. Each man would in turn provide the candles to play by, and as this house was said to be haunted, bedad they had it all to themselves. Well, this last night that ever they played there—it was Tom's own brother that told me this—just as they were going to deal the cards, a tall gentleman came out from a room that had been the kitchen. He walked right up to them—he was dressed in black cloth clothes, and wore a high black hat—and came right between two of the men and told them to deal out the cards. They were too frightened even to speak, so the stranger took the cards himself and dealt around to each man. And afterward he played with them; then he looked at every man in turn and walked out of the room. As soon as he cleared out of the place, the men all went away as quick as ever they could, and didn't stop to put out the lights. Each man cleared with himself and never stopped to look behind. And no one cared to play cards in that house afterward any more. That was Tom's own brother; and now the poor young man who was going home at midnight saw a light in one of the houses by the road, so he turned toward it, thinking to light his pipe. Just before knocking, he looked in at the window. As soon as he peeped in the light went out on him, and still he could see crowds of people, as thick as grass, just as you see 'em at a fair—so thick they hadn't room to stand—and they kept swaying back and forth, courtesying like. The kitchen was full, and looking through a door he saw a lot more of fine ladies and gentlemen; they were laughing and having great fun, running round the table setting out cups and saucers, just as if they were having a ball. Just then a big side-board fell over with a great crash, and all the fine people scampered away, and all was dark. So he turned away on his heel and was so frightened, his mother said, he could hardly get home from fear, and he had three whole miles to go. Next day he was thrashing corn in the barn and something upset him and pitched him head foremost across the flail. He rose, and three times he was pitched like that across the flail, so he gave up and went home. His mother asked him: 'Johnny, what is the matter with you? You do look very bad!' So he up and told her what had happened to him in the barn, and what he saw the night before. And he took suddenly sick and had to keep his bed for nine weeks, and when he got up and was walking around, he wasn't himself any more, and the sister says to the mother: 'Mother, I'm sure that it isn't Johnny that's there. It's only his shadow, for when I look at him, it isn't his features or face, but the face of another thing. He used to be so pleasant and cheerful, but now he looks like quite another man. Mother,' said she, 'we haven't Johnny at all.' Soon he got a little stronger and went to the capital town with corn. Several other men went also to get their corn ground. They were all coming home together a very cold night, and the men got up and sat on their sacks of corn. The other horses walked on all right with them, but Johnny's horses wouldn't move, not one step while he was on top of the load. Well, my dear, he called for the rest to come and help him—to see if the horses would go for them. But they would not move one step, though they whipped them and shouted at them to start on, for Johnny he was as heavy as lead. And he had to get down. Soon as he got down, the horses seemed glad and went off on a gallop after the rest of the train. So they all went off together, and Johnny wandered away into the bogs. His friends supposed, of course, he was coming on, thought he was walking beside his load; the snow was falling down, and perhaps they were a little afraid. He was left behind. They scoured the country for him next day, and, bedad, they found him, stiff dead, sitting against a fence. There's where they found him. They brought him on a door to his mother. Oh, it was a sad thing to see—to see her cry and hear her mourn!"

"And what more?" I asked.

"That's all. He was waked and buried, and that's what he got for playing cards! And that's all as true as ever could be true, for it's myself knew the old mother, and she told me it her very self, and she cried many tears for her son."

CHAPTER VII
DAILY DISTRACTIONS

But the sheep shearing came, and the hay season next, and then the harvest of small corn ... then the sweating of the apples, and the turning of the cider mill and the stacking of the firewood, and netting of the wood-cocks, and the springes to be mended in the garden and by the hedgerows, where the blackbirds hop to the molehills in the white October mornings and gray birds come to look for snails at the time when the sun is rising. It is wonderful how Time runs away when all these things, and a great many others, come in to load him down the hill, and prevent him from stopping to look about. And I, for my part, can never conceive how people who live in towns and cities, where neither lambs nor birds are (except in some shop windows), nor growing corn, nor meadow grass, nor even so much as a stick to cut, or a stile to climb and sit down upon—how these poor folk get through their lives without being utterly weary of them, and dying from pure indolence, is a thing God only knows, if his mercy allows him to think of it.

LORNA DOONE.

A farm-house looks on the outside like a quiet place. No men are seen about, front windows are closely shaded, front door locked. Go round to the back door; nobody seems to be at home. If by chance you do find, after long bruising of knuckles, that you have roused an inmate, it is some withered, sad-faced old dame, who is indifferent and hopelessly deaf, or a bare-footed, stupid urchin, who stares as if you had dropped from another planet, and a cool "Dunno" is the sole response to all inquiries.

All seems at a dead standstill. In reality everything and everybody is going at full speed, transpiring and perspiring to such a degree that, like a swiftly whirling top, it does not appear to move.

Friends think of me as not living, but simply existing, and marvel that I can endure such monotony. On the contrary, I live in a constant state of excitement, hurry, and necessity for immediate action.

The cows were continually getting out of pasture and into the corn; the pigs, like the chickens, evinced decided preference for the garden. The horse would break his halter and dart down the street, or, if in pasture, would leap the barbed-wire fence, at the risk of laming his legs for life, and dash into a neighbor's yard where children and babies were sunning on the grass.

Rival butchers and bakers would drive up simultaneously from different directions and plead for patronage and instant attention.

The vegetables must be gathered and carried to market; every animal was ravenously hungry at all hours, and didn't hesitate to speak of it. The magnificent peacock would wander off two miles, choosing the railroad track for his rambles, and loved to light on Si Evans's barn; then a boy must be detailed to recover the prize bird, said boy depending on a reward. His modest-hued consort would seek the deep hedges back of a distant swamp.

Friends would come from a distance to surprise and cheer me in my lonely retreat just at the time that the butter must positively be made, while the flowers were choking for water, smothered with weeds, "pus'ley," of course, pre-eminent. Then a book agent would appear, blind, but doubly persistent, with a five-dollar illustrated volume recounting minutely the Johnstown horror. And one of my dogs would be apt at this crisis to pursue and slay a chicken or poison himself with fly-paper. Every laboring man for miles around would come with an air of great importance to confidentially warn me against every other man that could be employed, with the stereotyped phrase in closing: "Well, whatever you do" (as if I might be left to do anything) "don't hire John Smallpate or Bill Storer. I've known him, man and boy, for thirty years; you'll do well not to trust *him!*"

Yet these same men who had so villified each other could be seen nightly lounging in front of the grocery, discussing politics and spitting in sweet unison.

The general animosity of my entire family to each other caused constant interruptions.

"Sandy," the handsome setter, loathed the pug, and tried to bite his neck in a fatal way. He also chased the rabbits, trod on young turkeys so that they were no more, drove the cat out of the barn and up a tree, barked madly at the cows, enraging those placid animals, and doted on frightening the horse.

The cat allowed mice to roam merrily through the grain bins, preferring robins and sparrows, especially young and happy mothers, to a proper diet; was fond of watching the chickens with wicked, malicious, greedy, dangerous eyes, and was always ready to make a sly spring for my canaries.

The rabbits (pretty innocent little creatures I had thought them, as I gazed at their representatives of white canton flannel, solidly stuffed, with such charming eyes of pink beads) girded all my young trees and killed them before I dreamed of such mischief, nibbled at every tender sprout, every swelling bud, were so agile that they could not be captured, and became such a maddening nuisance that I hired a boy to take them away. I fully understand the recent excitement of the Australians over the rabbit scourge which threatened to devastate their land.

The relations were strained between my cows; mother and daughter of a noble line; they always fed at opposite corners of the field, indulging in serious fights when they met.

My doves! I am almost ready to say that they were more annoying than all the rest of my motley collection, picked all seeds out of the ground faster than they could be put in, so large spaces sowed with rye lay bare all summer, and ate most of the corn and grain that was intended to fatten and stimulate my fowls.

Doves are poetical and pleasing, pigeons ditto—in literature, and at a safe distance from one's own barn. It's a pretty sight at sunset on a summer's eve to see them poising, wheeling, swirling, round a neighbor's barn. Their rainbow hues gleam brightly in the sun as they preen their feathers or gently "coo-oo, I love oo," on the ridge pole. I always longed to own some, but now the illusion is past. They have been admired and petted for ages, consecrated as emblems of innocence and peace and sanctity, regarded as almost sacred from the earliest antiquity. They have been idealized and praised from Noah to Anacreon, both inclined to inebriety! But in reality they are a dirty, destructive, greedy lot, and though fanciers sell them at high prices, they only command twenty-five cents per pair when sold for the market!

The hens lost half their feathers, often an eye, occasionally a life, in deadly feuds. My spunky little bantam game cock was always challenging one of my monster roosters and laying him low, so he had to be sent away.

John, my eccentric assistant, could abide no possible rival, insulted every man engaged to help him, occasionally indulging in a free fight after too frequent visits to the cider barrels of my next neighbor, so he had to follow the bantam.

Another distress was the constant calls of natives with the most undesirable things for me to buy; two or three calls daily for a long time. Boys with eager, ingenuous faces bringing carrier pigeons—pretty creatures—and I had been told there was money in pigeons. I paid them extortionate prices on account of extreme ignorance; and the birds, of course, flew home as soon as released, to be bought again by some gullible amateur. I had omitted to secure the names and addresses of these guileless lads.

A sandy-haired, lisping child with chronic catarrh offered me a lot of pet *rats!*

"I hear you like pets," she said, "Well, I've got some tame rats, a father and mother and thirteen little ones, and a mother with four. They're orful cunning. Hope you'll take 'em."

A big, red-faced, black-bearded, and determined man drove one day into the yard with an immense wagon, in which was standing a stupid, vicious old goat, and almost insisted on leaving it at a most ridiculously high price.

"Heard that the woman that had come to live here wanted most every animal that Noah got into the ark; was sure she'd like a goat." It was with considerable difficulty that he could be induced to take it away.

Dogs, dogs, dogs—from mastiff to mongrel, from St. Bernard to toy poodle—the yard really swarmed with them just before the first of May, when dog taxes must be paid!

A crow that could talk, but rather objectionably, was offered me.

A pert little boy, surrounded by his equally pert mates, said, after coming uninvited to look over my assortment: "Got most everything, hain't ye? Got a monkey?"

Then his satellites all giggled.

"No, not yet. Will not *you* come in?"

Second giggle, less hearty.

A superannuated clergyman walked three miles and a quarter in a heavy rain, minus umbrella, to bring me a large and common pitcher, badly cracked and of no original value; heard I was collecting old china. Then, after making a long call, drew out a tiny package from his vest pocket and offered for sale two time-worn cheap rings taken from his mother's dead hand. They were mere ghosts of rings that had once meant so much of joy or sorrow, pathetic souvenirs, one would think, to a loving son. He would also sell me his late father's old sermons for a good sum!

This reminded me of Sydney Smith's remark to an old lady who was sorely afflicted with insomnia: "Have you ever tried one of my sermons?"

Perhaps I have said enough to prove that life in a bucolic solitude may be something more varied than is generally—don't let that old peddler come into the house, say we want nothing, and then tell the ladies I'll be down directly—and, O *Ellen*, call Tom! Those ducks are devouring his new cabbage-plants and one of the calves has got over the stone wall and—what?

"He's gone to Dog Corner for the cow-doctor."

—Yes, more varied than is generally supposed!

CHAPTER VIII
THE PROSE OF NEW ENGLAND FARM LIFE

A life whose parlors have always been closed.

IK MARVEL.

Sunshine is tabooed in the front room of the house. The "damp dignity" of the best-room has been well described: "Musty smells, stiffness, angles, absence of sunlight. What is there to talk about in a room dark as the Domdaniel, except where one crack in a reluctant shutter reveals a stand of wax flowers under glass, and a dimly descried hostess who evidently waits only your departure to extinguish that solitary ray?"

At a recent auction I obtained twenty-one volumes of State Agricultural Reports for seventeen cents; and what I read in them of the Advantages of Rural Pursuits, The Dignity of Labor, The Relation of Agriculture to Longevity and to Nations, and, above all, of the Golden Egg, seem decidedly florid, unpractical, misleading, and very little permanent popularity can be gained by such self-interested buncombe from these eloquent orators.

The idealized farmer, as he is depicted by these white-handed rhetoricians who, like John Paul, "would never lay hand to a plow, unless said plow should actually pursue him to a second story, and then lay hands on it only to throw it out of the window," and the phlegmatic, overworked, horny-handed tillers of the soil are no more alike than Fenimore Cooper's handsome, romantic, noble, and impressive red man of the forest and the actual Sioux or Apache, as regarded by the cowboy of the West.

It's all work, with no play and no proper pay, for Western competition now prevents all chance of decent profits. Little can be laid up for old age, except by the most painful economy and daily scrimping; and how can the children consent to stay on, starving body and soul? *That* explains the 3,318 abandoned farms in Maine at present. And the farmers' wives! what monotonous, treadmill lives! Constant toil with no wages, no allowance, no pocket money, no vacations, no pleasure trips to the city nearest them, little of the pleasures of correspondence; no time to write, unless a near relative is dead or dying. Some one says that their only chance for social life is in going to some insane asylum! There have been four cases of suicide in farmers' families near me within eighteen months.

This does not apply to the fortunate farmer who inherited money and is shrewd enough to keep and increase it. Nor to the market gardener, who raises vegetables under glass; nor to the owners of large nurseries. These do make a good living, and are also able to save something.

In general, it is all one steady rush of work from March to November; unceasing, uncomplaining activity for the barest support, followed by three months of hibernation and caring for the cattle. Horace Greeley said: "If our most energetic farmers would abstract ten hours each per week from their incessant drudgery and devote them to reading and reflection in regard to their noble calling, they would live to a better purpose and bequeath better examples to their children."

It may have been true long years ago that no shares, factory, bank, or railroad paid better dividends than the plowshare, but it is the veriest nonsense now.

Think of the New England climate in summer. Rufus Choate describes it eloquently: "Take the climate of New England in summer, hot to-day, cold to-morrow, mercury at eighty degrees in the shade in the morning, with a sultry wind southwest. In three hours more a sea turn, wind at east, a thick fog from the bottom of the ocean, and a fall of forty degrees. Now so dry as to kill all the beans in New Hampshire, then floods carrying off all the dams and bridges on the Penobscot and Androscoggin. Snow in Portsmouth in July, and the next day a man and a yoke of oxen killed by lightning in Rhode Island. You would think the world was coming to an end. But we go along. Seed time and harvest never fail. We have the early and the latter rains; the sixty days of hot corn weather are pretty sure to be measured out to us; the Indian summer, with its bland south winds and mitigated sunshine, brings all up, and about the 25th of November, being Thursday, a grateful people gather about the Thanksgiving board, with hearts full of gratitude for the blessings that have been vouchsafed to them."

Poets love to sing of the sympathy of Nature. I think she is decidedly at odds with the farming interests of the country. At any rate, her antipathy to me was something intense and personal. That mysterious stepmother of ours was really riled by my experiments and determined to circumvent every agricultural ambition.

She detailed a bug for every root, worms to build nests on every tree, others to devour every leaf, insects to attack every flower, drought or deluge to ruin the crops, grasshoppers to finish everything that was left.

Potato bugs swooped down on my fields by tens of thousands, and when somewhat thinned in ranks by my unceasing war, would be re-enforced from a neighbor's fields, once actually fording my lakelet to get to my precious potato patch. The number and variety of devouring pests connected with each vegetable are alarming. Here are a few connected closely with the homely cabbage, as given by a noted helminthologist under the head of "Cut-worms":

"Granulated," "shagreened," "white," "marked," "greasy," "glassy," "speckled," "variegated," "wavy," "striped," "harlequin," "imbricated," "tarnished." The "snout beetle" is also a deadly foe.

To realize this horror, this worse than Pharaoh plague, you must either try a season of farming or peruse octavo volumes on Insects injurious to Vegetation, fully illustrated.

In those you may gain a faint idea of the "skippers," "stingers," "soothsayers," "walking sticks or specters," "saw flies and slugs," "boring caterpillars," "horn-tailed wood wasps," etc., etc., etc., etc.—a never-ending list. The average absolute loss of the farmers of this country from such pests is fully one million dollars per annum.

Gail Hamilton said of her squashes:

"They appeared above-ground, large-lobed and vigorous. Large and vigorous appeared the bugs, all gleaming in green and gold, like the wolf on the fold, and stopped up all the stomata and ate up all the parenchyma, till my squash-leaves looked as if they had grown for the sole purpose of illustrating net-veined organizations. A universal bug does not indicate a special want of skill in any one."

Not liking to crush the bug between thumb and finger as advised, she tried drowning them. She says: "The moment they touched the water they all spread unseen wings and flew away. I should not have been much more surprised to see Halicarnassus soaring over the ridge pole. I had not the slightest idea they could fly."

Then the aphides! Exhausters of strength—vine fretters—plant destroyers! One aphis, often the progenitor of over five thousand million aphides in a single season. This seems understated, but I accept it as the aphidavit of another noted helminthologist. I might have imagined Nature had a special grudge against me if I had not recalled Emerson's experience. He says: "With brow bent, with firm intent, I go musing in the garden walk. I stoop to pick up a weed that is choking the corn, find there were two; close behind is a third, and I reach out my arm to a fourth; behind that there are four thousand and one!

"Rose bugs and wasps appear best when flying. I admired them most when flying away from my garden."

Horace Greeley said that "No man who harbors caterpillars has any moral right to apples." But one sees whole orchards destroyed in this way for lack of time to attack such a big job. Farmers have been unjustly attacked by city critics who do not understand the situation. There was much fine writing last year in regard to the sin and shame of cutting down the pretty, wild growth of shrubs, vines, and flowers along the wayside, so picturesque to the summer tourist. The tangle of wild grape, clematis, and woodbine is certainly pretty, but underneath is sure to be found a luxuriant growth of thistle, wild carrot, silk weed, mullein, chickweed, tansy, and plantain, which, if allowed to seed and disseminate themselves, would soon ruin the best farms. There is a deadly foe, an army of foes, hiding under these luxuriant festoons and masses of cheerful flowers.

Isn't it strange and sad and pitiful, that it is the summer guest who alone enjoys the delights of summering in the country? There is no time for rest, for recreation, for flowers, for outdoor pleasures, for the average farmer and his family. You seldom see any bright faces at the windows, which are seldom opened—only a glimpse here and there of a sad, haggard creature, peering out for curosity. Strange would it be to hear peals of merry laughter; stranger still to see a family enjoying a meal on the piazza or a game on the grass. As for flowers, they are valued no more than weeds; the names of the most common are unknown. I asked in vain a dozen people last summer, what that flower was called, pointing to the ubiquitous Joe Rye weed or pink motherwort. At last I asked one man, who affected to know everything—

"Oh, yes, I know it."

"What is it?" I persisted.

"Well, I know it just as well, but can't just now get the name out." A pause, then, with great superiority: "I'd rather see a potato field in full bloom, than all the flowers in the world."

Perhaps some of Tolstoi's disciples may yet solve the problem of New England's abandoned farms. He believes that every able-bodied man should labor with his own hands and in "the sweat of his brow" to produce his own living direct from the soil. He dignifies agriculture above all other means of earning a living, and would have artificial employments given up. "Back to the land," he cries; and back he really goes, daily working with the peasants. But 'tis a solemn, almost tragical experience, not much better than the fate of the Siberian exile. Rise at dawn; work till dark; eat—go to bed too tired to read a paper;—and no money in it.

Let these once prosperous farms be given up to Swedish colonies, hard working and industrious, who can do better here than in their own country and have plenty of social life among themselves, or let wealthy men purchase half a dozen of these places to make a park, or two score for a hunting ground—or let unattached women of middle age occupy them and support themselves by raising poultry. Men are making handsome incomes from this business—women can do the same. The language of the poultry magazines, by the way, is equally sentimental and efflorescent with that of the speeches at agricultural fairs, sufficiently so to sicken one who has once accepted it as reliable, as for instance: "The individual must be very abnormal in his tastes if they can not be catered to by our feathered tribe." "To their owner they are a thing of beauty and a joy forever. Their ways are interesting, their language fascinating, and their lives from the egg to the mature fowl replete with constant surprises."[1]

Footnote 1: This clause is true.

"To simply watch them as they pass from stage to stage of development fills the mind of every sane person with pleasure." One poultry crank insists that each hen must be so carefully studied that she can be understood and managed as an individual, and speaks of his hens having at times an "anxious nervous expression!"

"Yes, it is where the hens sing all the day long in the barn-yard that throws off the stiff ways of our modern civilization and makes us feel that we are home and can rest and play and grow young once more. How many men and women have regained lost health and spirits in keeping hens, in the excitement of finding and gathering eggs!"

"It is not the natural laying season when snows lie deep on field and hill, when the frost tingles in sparkling beads from every twig, when the clear streams bear up groups of merry skaters," etc.

After my pathetic experience with chickens, who after a few days of downy content grew ill, and gasped until they gave up the ghost; ducklings, who progressed finely for several weeks, then turned over on their backs and flopped helplessly unto the end; or, surviving that critical period, were found in the drinking trough, "drowned, dead, because they couldn't keep their heads above water"; turkeys who flourished to a certain age, then grew feeble and phantom-like and faded out of life, I weary of gallinaceous rhodomontade, and crave "pointers" for my actual needs.

I still read "Crankin's" circulars with a thrill of enthusiasm because his facts are so cheering. For instance, from his latest: "We have some six thousand ducklings out now, confined in yards with wire netting eighteen inches high. The first lot went to market May 10th and netted forty cents per pound. These ducklings were ten weeks old and dressed on an average eleven pounds per pair. One pair dressed fourteen pounds." Isn't that better than selling milk at two and a half cents per quart? And no money can be made on vegetables unless they are raised under glass in advance of the season. I know, for did I not begin with "pie plant," with which every market was glutted, at one cent per pound, and try the entire list, with disgustingly low prices, exposed to depressing comparison and criticism? When endeavoring to sell, one of the visiting butchers, in reply to my petition that he would buy some of my vegetables, said: "Well now, Marm, you see just how it is; I've got more'n I can sell now, and women keep offering more all the way along. I tell 'em I can't buy 'em, but I'll *haul 'em off for ye* if ye want to get rid of 'em!" So much for market gardening at a distance from city demands.

But ducks! Sydney Smith, at the close of his life, said he "had but one illusion left, and that was the Archbishop of Canterbury." I still believe in Crankin and duck raising. Let me see: "One pair dressed fourteen pounds, netted forty cents per pound." I'll order one of Crankin's "Monarch" incubators and begin a poultry farm anew.

"*Dido et dux*," and so do Boston epicures. I'll sell at private sales, not for hotels! I used to imagine myself supplying one of the large hotels and saw on the *menu*:

"Tame duck and apple sauce (from the famous 'Breezy Meadows' farm)." But I inquired of one of the proprietors what he would give, and "fifteen cents per pound for poultry dressed and delivered" gave me a combined attack of chills and hysterics.

Think of *my* chickens, from those prize hens (three dollars each)—*my* chickens, fed on eggs hard boiled, milk, Indian meal, cracked corn, sun-flower seed, oats, buckwheat, the best of bread, selling at fifteen cents per pound, and I to pay express charges! Is there, is there any "money in hens?"

To show how a child would revel in a little rational enjoyment on a farm, read this dear little poem of James Whitcomb Riley's:

AT AUNTY'S HOUSE.

One time when we's at aunty's house—
    'Way in the country—where
They's ist but woods and pigs and cows,
    An' all's outdoors and air!
An orchurd swing; an' churry trees,
    An' *churries* in 'em! Yes, an' these
Here red-head birds steal all they please
    An' tech 'em if you dare!
W'y wunst, one time when we wuz there,
    We et out on the porch!

Wite where the cellar door wuz shut
    The table wuz; an' I
Let aunty set by me an' cut
    My wittles up—an' pie.
Tuz awful funny! I could see
    The red heads in the churry tree;
An' bee-hives, where you got to be
    So keerful going by;
An' comp'ny there an' all! An' we—
    We et out on the porch!

An'—I ist et *p'surves* an' things
    'At ma don't 'low me to—
An' chickun gizzurds (don't like wings
    Like parunts does, do you?)
An' all the time the wind blowed there

An' I could feel it in my hair,
An' ist smell clover ever'where!
   An' a old red head flew
Purt' nigh wite over my high chair,
   When we et out on the porch!

CHAPTER IX
THE PASSING OF THE PEACOCKS

I would rather look at a peacock than eat him. The feathers of an angel and the voice of a devil.

The story of this farm would not be complete without a brief rehearsal of my experiences, exciting, varied, and tragic, resulting from the purchase of a magnificent pair of peacocks.

My honest intention on leasing my forty-dollars-a-year paradise was simply to occupy the quaint old house for a season or two as a relief from the usual summer wanderings. I would plant nothing but a few hardy flowers of the old-fashioned kind—an economical and prolonged picnic. In this way I could easily save in three years sufficient funds to make a grand *tour du monde*.

That was my plan!

For some weeks I carried out this resolution, until an event occurred, which changed the entire current of thought, and transformed a quiet, rural retreat into a scene of frantic activity and gigantic undertaking.

In the early summer I attended a poultry show at Rooster, Mass., and, in a moment of impulsive enthusiasm, was so foolish as to pause and admire and long for a prize peacock, until I was fairly and hopelessly hypnotized by its brilliant plumage.

I reasoned: Anybody can keep hens, "me and Crankin" can raise ducks, geese thrive naturally with me, but a peacock is a rare and glorious possession. The proud scenes he is associated with in mythology, history, and art rushed through my mind with whirlwind rapidity as I stood debating the question. The favorite bird of Juno—she called the metallic spots on its tail the eyes of Argus—imported by Solomon to Palestine, essentially regal. Kings have used peacocks as their crests, have worn crowns of their feathers. Queens and princesses have flirted gorgeous peacock fans; the pavan, a favorite dance in the days of Louis le Grand, imitated its stately step. In the days of chivalry the most solemn oath was taken on the peacock's body, roasted whole and adorned with its gay feathers, as Shallow swore "by cock and pie." I saw the fairest of all the fair dames at a grand mediaeval banquet proudly bearing the bird to the table. The woman who hesitates is lost. I bought the pair, and ordered them boxed for "Breezy Meadows."

On the arrival of the royal pair at my 'umble home, all its surroundings began to lose the charm of rustic simplicity, and appear shabby, inappropriate, and unendurable. It became evident that the entire place must be raised, and at once, to the level of those peacocks.

The house and barn were painted (colonial yellow) without a moment's delay. An ornamental piazza was added, all the paths were broadened and graveled, and even terraces were dreamed of, as I recalled the terraces where Lord Beaconsfield's peacocks used to sun themselves and display their beauties—Queen Victoria now has a screen made of their feathers.

My expensive pets felt their degradation in spite of my best efforts and determined to sever their connection with such a plebeian place.

Beauty (I ought to have called him Absalom or Alcibiades), as soon as let out of his traveling box, displayed to an admiring crowd a tail so long it might be called a "serial," gave one contemptuous glance at the premises, and departed so rapidly, by running and occasional flights, that three men and a boy were unable to catch up with him for several hours. Belle was not allowed her liberty, as we saw more trouble ahead. A large yard, inclosed top and sides with wire netting, at last restrained their roving ambition. But they were not happy. Peacocks disdain a "roost" and seek the top of some tall tree; they are also rovers by nature and hate confinement. They pined and failed, and seemed slowly dying; so I had to let them out. Total cost of peacock hunts by the boys of the village, $11.33. I found that Beauty was happy only when admiring himself, or deep in mischief. His chief delight was to mount the stone wall, and utter his raucous note, again and again, as a carriage passed, often scaring the horses into dangerous antics, and causing severe, if not profane criticism. Or he would steal slyly into a neighbor's barn and kill half a dozen chickens at a time. He was awake every morning by four o'clock, and would announce the glories of the coming dawn by a series of ear-splitting notes, disturbing not only all my guests, but the various families within range, until complaints and petitions were sent in. He became a nuisance—but how could he be muzzled?

And he was so gloriously handsome! Visitors from town would come expressly to see him. School children would troop into my yard on Saturday afternoons, "to see the peacock spread his tail," which he often capriciously refused to do. As soon as they departed, somewhat disappointed in "my great moral show," Beauty would go to a large window on the ground floor of the barn and parade up and down, displaying his beauties for his own gratification. At last he fancied he saw a rival in this brilliant, irridescent reflection and pecked fiercely at the glass, breaking several panes.

Utterly selfish, he would keep all dainty bits for himself, leaving the scraps for his devoted mate, who would wait meekly to eat what he chose to leave. She made up for this wifely self-abnegation by frequenting the hen houses. She would watch patiently by the side of a hen on her nest, and as soon as an egg was deposited, would remove it for her luncheon. She liked raw eggs, and six were her usual limit.

There is a deal of something closely akin to human nature in barnyard fowls. It was irresistibly ludicrous to see the peacock strutting about in the sunshine, his tail expanded in fullest glory, making a curious rattle of triumph as he paraded, while my large white Holland turkey gobbler, who had been molting severely and was almost denuded as to tail feathers, would attempt to emulate his display, and would follow him closely, his wattles swelling and reddening with fancied success, making all this fuss about what had been a fine array, but now was reduced to five scrubby, ragged, very dirty remnants of feathers. He fancied himself equally fine, and was therefore equally happy.

Next came the molting period.

Pliny said long ago of the peacock: "When he hath lost his taile, he hath no delight to come abroad," but I knew nothing of this peculiarity, supposing that a peacock's tail, once grown, was a permanent ornament. On the contrary, if a peacock should live one hundred and twenty years (and his longevity is something phenomenal) he would have one hundred and seventeen new and interesting tails—enough to start a circulating library. Yes, Beauty's pride and mine had a sad fall as one by one the long plumes were dropped in road and field and garden. He should have been caught and confined, and the feathers, all loose at once, should have been pulled out at one big pull and saved intact for fans and dust brushes, and adornment of mirrors and fire-places. Soon every one was gone, and the mortified creature now hid away in the corn, and behind shrubbery, disappearing entirely from view, save as hunger necessitated a brief emerging.

This tailless absentee was not what I had bought as the champion prize winner. And Belle, after laying four eggs, refused to set. But I put them under a turkey, and, to console myself and re-enforce my position as an owner of peacocks, I began to study peacock lore and literature. I read once more of the throne of the greatest of all the moguls at Delhi, India.

"The under part of the canopy is embroidered with pearls and diamonds, with a fringe of pearls round about. On the top of the canopy, which is made like an arch with four panes, stands a peacock with his tail spread, consisting all of sapphires and other proper-colored stones; the body is of beaten gold enchased with several jewels, and a great ruby upon his breast, at which hangs a pearl that weighs fifty carats. On each side of the peacock stand two nosegays as high as the bird, consisting of several sorts of flowers, all of beaten gold enameled. When the king seats himself upon the throne, there is a transparent jewel with a diamond appendant, of eighty or ninety carats, encompassed with rubies and emeralds, so hung that it is always in his eye. The twelve pillars also that support the canopy are set with rows of fair pearls, round, and of an excellent water, that weigh from six to ten carats apiece. At the distance of four feet upon each side of the throne are placed two parasols or umbrellas, the handles whereof are about eight feet high, covered with diamonds; the parasols themselves are of crimson velvet, embroidered and stringed with pearls." This is the famous throne which Tamerlane began and Shah Jahan finished, which is really reported to have cost a hundred and sixty million five hundred thousand livres (thirty-two million one hundred thousand dollars).

I also gloated over the description of that famous London dining-room, known to the art world as the "Peacock Room," designed by Whistler. Panels to the right and left represent peacocks with their tails spread fan-wise, advancing in perspective toward the spectator, one behind the other, the peacocks in gold and the ground in blue.

I could not go so extensively into interior decoration, and my mania for making the outside of the house and the grounds highly decorative had received a severe lesson in the verdict, overheard by me, as I stood in the garden, made by a gawky country couple who were out for a Sunday drive.

As Warner once said to me, "young love in the country is a very solemn thing," and this shy, serious pair slowed up as they passed, to see my place. The piazza was gay with hanging baskets, vines, strings of beads and bells, lanterns of all hues; there were tables, little and big, and lounging chairs and a hammock and two canaries. The brightest geraniums blossomed in small beds through the grass, and several long flower beds were one brilliant mass of bloom, while giant sun-flowers reared their golden heads the entire length of the farm.

It was gay, but I had hoped to please Beauty.

"What is that?" said the girl, straining her head out of the carriage.

"Don't know," said the youth, "guess it's a store."

The girl scrutinized the scene as a whole, and said decisively:

"No, 'taint, Bill—it's a saloon!"

That was a cruel blow! I forgot my flowers, walked in slowly and sadly and carried in two lanterns to store in the shed chamber. I also resolved to have no more flower beds in front of the house, star shaped or diamond—they must all be sodded over.

That opinion of my earnest efforts to effect a renaissance at Gooseville—to show how a happy farm home should look to the passer-by—in short, my struggle to "live up to" the peacocks revealed, as does a lightning flash on a dark night, much that I had not perceived. I had made as great a mistake as the farmer who abjures flowers and despises "fixin' up."

The pendulum of emotion swung as far back, and I almost disliked the innocent cause of my decorative folly. I began to look over my accounts, to study my check books, to do some big sums in addition, and it made me even more depressed. Result of these mental exercises as follows: Rent, $40 per year; incidental expenses to date, $5,713.85. Was there any good in this silly investment of mine? Well, if it came to the very worst, I could kill the couple and have a rare dish. Yet Horace did not think its flesh equal to an ordinary chicken. He wrote:

I shall ne'er prevail

To make our men of taste a pullet choose,

And the gay peacock with its train refuse.

For the rare bird at mighty price is sold,

And lo! What wonders from its tail unfold!

But can these whims a higher gusto raise

Unless you eat the plumage that you praise?

Or do its glories when 'tis boiled remain?

No; 'tis the unequaled beauty of its train,

Deludes your eye and charms you to the feast,

For hens and peacocks are alike in taste.

Then peacocks have been made useful in a medicinal way. The doctors once prescribed peacock broth for pleurisy, peacocks' tongues for epilepsy, peacocks' fat for colic, peacocks' galls for weak eyes, peahens' eggs for gout.

It is always darkest just before dawn, and only a week from that humiliating Sunday episode I was called by my gardener to look at the dearest little brown something that was darting about in the poultry yard. It was a baby peacock, only one day old. He got out of the nest in some way, and preferred to take care of himself. How independent, how captivating he was! As not one other egg had hatched, he was lamentably, desperately alone, with dangers on every side, "homeless and orphanless." Something on that Sabbath morning recalled Melchizedec, the priest without father or mother, of royal descent, and of great length of days. Earnestly hoping for longevity for this feathered mite of princely birth, I called him "Melchizedec."

I caught him and was in his toils. He was a tiny tyrant; I was but a slave, an attendant, a nurse, a night-watcher. Completely under his claw!

No more work, no more leisure, no more music or tennis; my life career, my sphere, was definitely settled. I was Kizzie's attendant—nothing more. People have cared for rather odd pets, as the leeches tamed and trained by Lord Erskine; others have been deeply interested in toads, crickets, mice, lizards, alligators, tortoises, and monkeys. Wolsey was on familiar terms with a venerable carp; Clive owned a pet tortoise; Sir John Lubbock contrived to win the affections of a Syrian wasp; Charles Dudley Warner devoted an entire article in the Atlantic Monthly to the praises of his cat Calvin; but did you ever hear of a peacock as a household pet?

As it is the correct thing now to lie down all of a summer afternoon, hidden by trees, and closely watch every movement of a pair of little birds, or spend hours by a frog pond studying the sluggish life there, and as mothers are urged by scientific students to record daily the development of their infants in each apparently unimportant matter, I think I may be excused for a brief sketch of my charge, for no mother ever had a child so precocious, so wise, so willful, so affectionate, so persistent, as Kizzie *at the same age*. Before he was three days old, he would follow me like a dog up and down stairs and all over the house, walk behind me as I strolled about the grounds, and when tired, he would cry and "peep, weep" for me to sit down. Then he would beg to be taken on my lap, thence he would proceed to my arm, then my neck, where he would peck and scream and flutter, determined to nestle there for a nap. My solicitude increased as he lived on, and I hoped to "raise" him. He literally demanded every moment of my time, my entire attention during the day, and, alas! at night also, until I seemed to be living a tragic farce!

If put down on carpet or matting, he at once began to pick up everything he could spy on the floor, and never before did I realize how much could be found there. I had a dressmaker in the house, and Kizzie was always going for a deadly danger—here a pin, there a needle, just a step away a tack or a bit of thread or a bead of jet.

Outdoors it was even worse. With two bird dogs ready for anything but birds, the pug that had already devoured all that had come to me of my expensive importations, a neighbor's cat often stealing over to hunt for her dinner, a crisis seemed imminent every minute. Even his own father would destroy him if they met, as the peacock allows no possible rival. And Kizzie kept so close to my heels that I hardly dared step. If my days were distracting, the nights were inexpressibly awful. I supposed he would be glad to go to sleep in a natural way after a busy day. No, indeed! He would not stay in box or basket, or anywhere but cradled close in my neck. There he wished to remain, twittering happily, giving now and then a sweet, little, tremulous trill, indicative of content, warmth, and drowsiness; if I dared to move ever so little, showing by a sharp scratch from his claws that he preferred absolute quiet. One night, when all worn out, I rose and put him in a hat box and covered it closely, but his piercing cries of distress and anger prevented the briefest nap, reminding me of the old man who said, "Yes, it's pretty dangerous livin' anywheres." I was so afraid of hurting him that I scarcely dared move. Each night we had a prolonged battle, but he never gave in for one instant until he could roost on my outstretched finger or just under my chin. Then he would settle down, the conflict over, he as usual the victor, and the sweet little lullaby would begin.

One night I rose hastily to close the windows in a sudden shower. Kizzie wakened promptly, and actually followed me out of the room and down-stairs. Alas! it was not far from his breakfast hour, for he preferred his first meal at four o'clock A.M. You see how he influenced me to rise early and take plenty of exercise.

I once heard of a wealthy Frenchman, nervous and dyspeptic, who was ordered by his eccentric physician to buy a Barbary ostrich and imitate him as well as care for him. And he was quickly cured!

On the other hand, it is said that animals and birds grow to be like those who train and pet them. Christopher North (John Wilson) used to carry a sparrow in his coat pocket. And his friends averred that the bird grew so large and impressive that it seemed to be changing into an *eagle*.

But Kizzie was the stronger influence. I really grew afraid of him, as he liked to watch my eyes, and once picked at them, as he always picked at any shining bit.

What respect I now feel for a sober, steady-going, successful old hen, who raises brood after brood of downy darlings without mishaps! Her instinct is an inspiration. Kizzie liked to perch on my finger and catch flies for his dinner. How solemn, wise, and bewitching he did look as he snapped at and swallowed fifteen flies, uttering all the time a satisfied little note, quite distinct from his musical slumber song!

How he enjoyed lying on one side, stretched out at full length, to bask in the sun, a miniature copy of his magnificent father! Very careful was he of his personal appearance, pruning and preening his pretty feathers many times each day, paying special attention to his tail—not more than an inch long—but what a prophecy of the future! As mothers care most for the most troublesome child, so I grew daily more fond of cute little Kizzie, more anxious that he should live.

I could talk all day of his funny ways, of his fondness for me, of his daily increasing intelligence, of his hair-breadth escapes, etc.

The old story—the dear gazelle experience came all too soon.

Completely worn out with my constant vigils, I intrusted him for one night to a friend who assured me that she was a most quiet sleeper, and that he could rest safely on her fingers. I was too tired to say no.

She came to me at daybreak, with poor Kizzie dead in her hands. He died like Desdemona, smothered with pillows. All I can do in his honor has been done by this inadequate recital of his charms and his capacity. After a few days of sincere grief I reflected philosophically that if he had not passed away I must have gone soon, and naturally felt it preferable that I should be the survivor.

A skillful taxidermist has preserved as much of Kizzie as possible for me, and he now adorns the parlor mantel, a weak, mute reminder of three weeks of anxiety.

And his parents—

The peahen died suddenly and mysteriously. There was no apparent reason for her demise, but the autopsy, which revealed a large and irregular fragment of window glass lodged in her gizzard, proved that she was a victim of Beauty's vanity. A friend who was present said, as he tenderly held the glass between thumb and finger: "It is now easy to see through the cause of her death; under the circumstances, it would be idle to speak of it as pane-less!" Beauty had never seemed very devoted to her, but he mourned her long and sincerely. Now that she had gone he appreciated her meek adoration, her altruistic devotion.

Another touch like human nature.

And when, after a decent period of mourning, another spouse was secured for him he refused to notice her and wandered solitary and sad to a neighbor's fields. The new madam was not allowed to share the high roost on the elm. She was obliged to seek a less elevated and airy dormitory. His voice, always distressingly harsh, was now so awful that it was fascinating. The notes seemed cracked by grief or illness. At last, growing feebler, he succumbed to some wasting malady and no longer strutted about in brilliant pre-eminence or came to the piazza calling imperiously for dainties, but rested for hours in some quiet corner. The physician who was called in prescribed for his liver. He showed symptoms of poisoning, and I began to fear that in his visit to a neighbor's potato fields he had indulged in Paris green, possibly with suicidal intent.

There was something heroic in his way of dying. No moans, no cries; just a dignified endurance. From the western window of the shed chamber where he lay he could see the multitude of fowls below, in the yards where he had so lately reigned supreme. Occasionally, with a heroic effort, he would get on his legs and gaze wistfully on the lively crowd so unmindful of his wretchedness, then sink back exhausted, reminding me of some grand old monarch, statesman, or warrior looking for the last time on the scenes of his former triumphs. I should have named him Socrates. At last he was carried to a cool resting place in the deep grass, covered with pink mosquito netting, and one kind friend after another fanned him and watched over his last moments. After he was really dead, and Tom with tears rolling down his face carried him tenderly away, I woke from my ambitious dream and felt verily guilty of aviscide.

But for my vainglorious ambition Beauty would doubtless be alive and resplendent; his consort, modest hued and devoted, at his side, and my bank account would have a better showing.

There is a motto as follows, "Let him keep peacock to himself," derived in this way:

When George III had partly recovered from one of his attacks, his ministers got him to read the king's speech, but he ended every sentence with the word "peacock."

The minister who drilled him said that "peacock" was an excellent word for ending a sentence, only kings should not let subjects hear it, but should whisper it softly.

The result was a perfect success; the pause at the close of each sentence had such a fine elocutionary effect.

In future, when longing to indulge in some new display, yield to another temptation, let me whisper "peacock" and be saved.

CHAPTER X
LOOKING BACK

Then you seriously suppose, doctor, that gardening is good for the constitution?

I do. For kings, lords, and commons. Grow your own cabbages. Sow your own turnips, and if you wish for a gray head, cultivate carrots.

THOMAS HOOD.

Conceit is not encouraged in the country. Your level is decided for you, and the public opinion is soon reported as something you should know.

As a witty spinster once remarked: "It's no use to fib about your age in your native village. Some old woman always had a calf born the same night you were!"

Jake Corey was refreshingly frank. He would give me a quizzical look, shift his quid, and begin:

"Spent a sight o' money on hens, hain't ye? Wall, by next year I guess you'll find out whether ye want to quit foolin' with hens or not. Now, my hens doan't git no condition powder, nor sun-flower seeds, nor no such nonsense, and I ain't got no bone cutter nor fancy fountains for 'em; but I let 'em scratch for themselves and have their liberty, and mine look full better'n your'n. I'll give ye one p'int. You could save a lot by engagin' an old hoss that's got to be killed. I'm allers looking round in the fall of the year for some old critter just ready to drop. Wait till cold weather, and then, when he's killed, hang half of him up in the hen house and see how they'll pick at it. It's the best feed going for hens, and makes 'em lay right along. Doan't cost nothin' either."

I had been asked to give a lecture in a neighboring town, and, to change the subject, inquired if he thought many would attend. Jake looked rather blank, took off his cap, scratched his head, and then said:

"I dunno. Ef you was a Beecher or a Gough you could fill the hall, or may be ef your more known like, and would talk to 'em free, you might git 'em, or if you's going to sing or dress up to make 'em larf; but as *'tis*, I dunno." After the effort was over I tried to sound him as to my success. He was unusually reticent, and would only say: "Wall, the only man I heard speak on't, said 'twas different from anything he ever heard." This reminded me of a capital story told me by an old family doctor many years ago. It was that sort of anecdote now out of fashion with *raconteurs*—a long preamble, many details, a gradual increase of interest, and a vivid climax, and when told by a sick bed would sometimes weary the patient. A man not especially well known had given a lecture in a New Hampshire town without rousing much enthusiasm in his audience, and as he rode away on the top of the stage coach next morning he tried to get some sort of opinion from Jim Barker, the driver. After pumping in vain for a compliment the gentleman inquired: "Did you hear nothing about my lecture from any of the people? I should like very much to get some idea of how it was received."

"Wall, no, stranger, I can't say as I heerd much. I guess the folks was purty well pleased. No one seemed to be ag'in it but Square Lothrop."

"And may I ask what he said?"

"Wall, I wouldn't mind it, if I'se you, what he said. He says just what he thinks—right out with it, no matter who's hurt—and he usually gets the gist on't. But I wouldn't mind what he said, the public was purty generally pleased." And the long whip lash cracks and Jim shouts, "Get an, Dandy."

"Yes," persisted the tortured man; "but I do want very much to know what Squire Lothrop's opinion was."

"Now, stranger, I wouldn't think any more about the Square. He's got good common sense and allers hits the nail on the head, but as I said, you pleased 'em fust rate."

"Yes, but I must know what Squire Lothrop did say."

"Wall, if you will have it, he did say (and he's apt to get the gist on't) he did say that *he* thought 'twas *awful shaller!*"

Many epigrammatic sayings come back to me, and one is too good to be omitted, An old woman was fiercely criticising a neighbor and ended in this way: "Folks that pretend to be somebody, and don't act like nobody, ain't anybody!"

Another woman reminded me of Mrs. Partington. She told blood-curdling tales of the positive reappearance of departed spirits, and when I said, "Do you really believe all this?" she replied, "Indeed, I do, and yet I'm not an *imaginary* woman!" Her dog was provoked into a conflict with my setters, and she exclaimed: "Why, I never saw him so completely *ennervated.*"

Then the dear old lady who said she was a free thinker and wasn't ashamed of it; guessed she knew as much as the minister 'bout this world or the next; liked nothing better than to set down Sunday afternoons after she'd fed her hens and read Ingersoll. "What books of his have you?" I asked.

She handed me a small paper-bound volume which did not look like any of "Bob's" productions. It was a Guide Book through Picturesque Vermont by Ernest Ingersoll!

And I must not omit the queer sayings of a simple-hearted hired man on a friend's farm.

Oh, for a photo of him as I saw him one cold, rainy morning tending Jason Kibby's dozen cows. He had on a rubber coat and cap, but his trouser legs were rolled above the knee and he was barefoot, "Hannibal," I shouted, "you'll take cold with your feet in that wet grass!"

"Gueth not, Marm," he lisped back cheerily. "I never cared for shooth mythelf."

He was always shouting across the way to inquire if "*thith* wath hot enough or cold enough to thute *me*?" As if I had expressed a strong desire for phenomenal extremes of temperature. One morning he suddenly departed. I met him trudging along with three hats jammed on to his head and a rubber coat under his arm, for 'twas a fine day.

"Why, Hanny!" I exclaimed, "where are you going in such haste?"

"Mithter Kibby told me to go to Halifax, and—I'm going!"

Next, the man who was anxious to go into partnership with me. He would work my farm at halves, or I could buy his farm, cranberry bog, and woodland, and he would live right on there and run that place at halves; urged me to buy twelve or fourteen cows cheap in the fall and start a milk route, he to be the active partner; then he had a chance to buy a lot of "essences" cheap, and if I'd purchase a peddling-wagon, he'd put in his old horse, and we'd go halves on that business, or I could buy up a lot of calves or young pigs and he'd feed 'em and we'd go halves.

But I will not take you through my entire picture-gallery, as I have two good stories to tell you before saying good-by.

Depressing remarks have reached me about my "lakelet," which at first was ridiculed by every one. The struggle of evolution from the "spring hole" was severe and protracted. Experts were summoned, their estimates of cost ranging from four hundred to one thousand dollars, and no one thought it worth while to touch it. It was discouraging. Venerable and enormous turtles hid in its muddy depths and snapped at the legs of the ducks as they dived, adding a limp to the waddle; frogs croaked there dismally; mosquitoes made it a camping ground and head center; big black water snakes often came to drink and lingered by the edge; the ugly horn pout was the only fish that could live there. Depressing, in contrast with my rosy dreams! But now the little lake is a charming reality, and the boat is built and launched. Turtles, pout, lily roots as big as small trees, and two hundred loads of "alluvial deposit" are no longer "in it," while carp are promised me by my friend Commissioner Blackford. The "Tomtoolan"[2] is not a large body of water—one hundred and fifty feet long, seventy-five feet wide—but it is a delight to me and has been grossly traduced by ignorant or envious outsiders. The day after the "Katy-Did" was christened (a flat-bottomed boat, painted prettily with blue and gold) I invited a lady to try it with me. Flags were fluttering from stem and stern. We took a gayly colored horn to toot as we went, and two dippers to bail, if necessary. It was not exactly "Youth at the prow and Pleasure at the helm," but we were very jolly and not a little proud.

Footnote 2: Named in honor of the amateur engineers.

A neglected knot-hole soon caused the boat to leak badly. We had made but one circuit, when we were obliged to "hug the shore" and devote our entire energies to bailing. "Tip her a little more," I cried, and the next instant we were both rolled into the water. It was an absurd experience, and after scrambling out, our clothes so heavy we could scarcely step, we vowed, between hysteric fits of laughter, to keep our tip-over a profound secret.

But the next time I went to town, friends began to smile mysteriously, asked me if I had been out on the lake yet, made sly and jocose allusions to a sudden change to Baptistic faith, and if I cordially invited them to join me in a row, would declare a preference for surf and salt water, or, if pressed, would murmur in the meanest way something about having a bath-tub at home.

It is now nearly a year since that little adventure, but it is still a subject of mirth, even in other towns. A friend calling yesterday told me the version he had just heard at Gillford, ten miles away!

"You bet they have comical goings-on at that woman's farm by the Gooseville depot! She got a regular menagerie, fust off—everything she see or could hear of. Got sick o' the circus bizness, and went into potatoes deep. They say she was actually up and outdoors by daybreak, working and worrying over the tater bugs!

"She's a red-headed, fleshy woman, and some of our folks going by in the cars would tell of seeing her tramping up and down the long furrows, with half a dozen boys hired to help her. Soon as she'd killed most of her own, a million more just traveled over from the field opposite where they had had their own way and cleaned out most everything. Then, what the bugs spared, the long rains rotted. So I hear she's giv' up potatoes.

"Then she got sot on scooping out a seven by nine mud hole to make a pond, and had a boat built to match.

"Well, by darn, she took a stout woman in with her, and, as I heerd it, that boat just giv' one groan, and sunk right down!"

As to the potatoes, I might never have escaped from that terrific thralldom, if a city friend, after hearing my woful experience, had not inquired quietly:

"Why have potatoes? It's much cheaper to buy all you need!"

I had been laboring under a strange spell—supposed I *must* plant potatoes; the relief is unspeakable.

Jennie June once said, "The great art of life is to *eliminate*." I admired the condensed wisdom of this, but, like experience, it only serves to illume the path over which I have passed.

One little incident occurred this spring which is too funny to withhold. Among the groceries ordered from Boston was a piece of extra fine cheese. A connoisseur in cheese had advised me to try it. It recommended itself so strongly that I placed it carefully under glass, in a place all by itself. It *was* strong—strong enough to sew buttons on, strong as Sampson, strong enough to walk away alone. One warm morning it seemed to have gained during the night. Its penetrating, permeating power was something, almost supernatural. I carried it from one place to another, each time more remote. It would not be lonely if segregrated, doubtless it had ample social facilities within itself! At last I became desperate. "Ellen," I exclaimed, "just bring in that cheese and burn it. It comes high, too high. I can not endure it." She opened the top of the range and, as the cremation was going on, I continued my comments. "Why, in all my life, I never knew anything like it; wherever I put it—in pantry, swing cupboard, on the cellar stairs, in a tin box, on top of the refrigerator—way out on that—" Just then Tom opened the door and said:

"Miss, your fertilizer's come!"

I have told you of my mistakes, failures, losses, but have you any idea of my daily delights, my lasting gains?

From invalidism to health, from mental depression to exuberant spirits, that is the blessed record of two years of amateur farming. What has done this? Exercise, actual hard work, digging in the dirt.

We are made of dust, and the closer our companionship with Mother Earth in summer time the longer we shall keep above ground. Then the freedom from conventional restraints of dress; no necessity for "crimps," no need of foreign hirsute adornment, no dresses with tight arm holes and trailing skirts, no high-heeled slippers with pointed toes, but comfort, clear comfort, indoors and out.

Plenty of rocking chairs, lounges that make one sleepy just to look at them, open fires in every room, and nothing too fine for the sun to glorify; butter, eggs, cream, vegetables, poultry—simply perfect, and the rare, ecstatic privilege of eating onions—onions raw, boiled, baked, and fried at any hour or all hours. I said comfort; it is luxury!

Dr. Holmes says: "I have seen respectability and amiability grouped over the air-tight stove, I have seen virtue and intelligence hovering over the register, but I have never seen true happiness in a family circle where the faces were not illuminated by the blaze of an open fireplace." And nature! I could fill pages with glowing descriptions of Days Outdoors. In my own homely pasture I have found the dainty wild rose, the little field strawberries so fragrant and spicy, the blue berries high and low, so desirable for "pie-fodder," and daisies and ferns in abundance, and, in an adjoining meadow by the brookside, the cardinal flower and the blue gentian. All these simple pleasures seem better to me than sitting in heated, crowded rooms listening to interminable music, or to men or women who never know when to stop, or rushing round to gain more information on anything and everything from Alaska to Zululand, and wildly struggling to catch up with "social duties."

City friends, looking at the other side of the shield, marvel at my contentment, and regard me as buried alive. But when I go back for a short time to the old life I am fairly homesick. I miss my daily visit to the cows and the frolic with the dogs. All that has been unpleasant fades like a dream.

I think of the delicious morning hours on the broad vine-covered piazza, the evenings with their starry splendor or witching moonlight, the nights of sound sleep and refreshing rest, the all-day picnics, the jolly drives with friends as charmed with country life as myself, and I weary of social functions and overpowering intellectual privileges, and every other advantage of the metropolis, and long to migrate once more from Gotham to Gooseville.

"Dear country life of child and man!
    For both the best, the strongest,
That with the earliest race began,
    And hast outlived the longest,
Their cities perished long ago;
    Who the first farmers were we know."

THE END.

Milton Keynes UK
Ingram Content Group UK Ltd.
UKHW031031210324
439796UK00008B/673